Contents

PART ONE: Secretion

PART TWO: Excretion

One

Seems Like There's An Echo in the Room & Why Stupidity Matters

"Darling!" Sarah's mother crowed. "Guess who got the job of headmistress?!"

Sarah frowned and crossed her arms. "Mother, I'm not deaf. There's no need to repeat yourself. You've just said that twenty seconds ago." The dark-haired beauty stood, crooked, surveying the scene in front of her. "Er … I don't know. Who got the job as headmistress? You?" she scoffed.

Mrs Jones - Sam - chuckled heartily and sat herself on one of the rotating seats which the former headmaster Stuart Bates had so fondly admired. She swivelled around for a moment, and then straightened herself up. "Me? Don't be silly darling, why would I get the job as headmistress?"

Sarah swallowed hard. "Er, because you're standing - sitting - in the head's office in a suit, looking all posh and dapper like you own the place." She added, spotting two members of staff - Miller and Matthews, "And you've got two guard-dogs to watch over your things."

Sam Jones slapped a hand to her head. She swung around to face Dr Matthews and his sidekick, Miller. "Duh - she guessed! What a clever girl we have here! I've trained her well!" Another burst of laughter. "Doesn't fall for any tricks, does she? Hohoho!"

Her daughter narrowed her eyes, and only unfolded her arms so that she could tug ferociously at a lock of ebony hair which was falling in her face.

"Darling," her mother proclaimed, "you really ought to get that hair cut. Or tie it back. How on earth do you play sport with hair such a nuisance?"

"Er, they don't, Mrs Jones," Dr Matthews said, sounding a little like he had a poker stuck up his backside, when really the poker from the burning fire was only just inching into his crack. "Sport is optional in sixth-form. Optional in that you either don't do it, or you don't do it. Most pupils decide not to do it."

Sam touched her short, layered dark hair subconsciously. "I see. Well, we'll just have to see about that, then …"

"Wait a minute, wait a minute!" Sarah exclaimed loudly, cutting off the sound of a ticking, which Mr Miller presumed was his heart-beat. He sat down on the brown leather sofa, and tried to concentrate on not concentrating.

"I don't understand. Are you the bloody headmistress or aren't you?"

Sam Jones tinkled again. "Of course, silly! Anyone could see that!"

"My mother is turning into Bridget Jones's mother more and more every day I see her," Sarah moaned the following morning just before one of her English teachers, Mrs Macintosh, was due to turn up late to the lesson.

"Don't you mean Bridget James?" Talullaah Ali asked, surveying her long, perfectly manicured nails. "In the year below?"

"Why … what does Bridget James's mother do?"

The young Muslim girl let a smile flicker onto her face. "She's a bloody nutcase. Came rushing into school claiming that her daughter had been assaulted last year by Mr Bates and that she wanted to press charges, for some stupid reason." Talullaah snorted a little.

"Oh," Sarah exclaimed, "Bridget James? Talullaah, she was one of the victims of Mr Bates! She was in court the other Wednesday, whenever it was. Because I can't quite remember. I've got a bad memory. Anyway …" She cried,

"Her mother had all the rights in the world to come in and complain. But that's beside the point."

"What *was* your point?"

"Just like a serial novel, I'm not quite sure. Um … oh, yes. My mother. Hold on … haven't we already had English today?"

"Yeah, but it's your mother's idea of taking the piss. You do know she's headmistress, don't you?" Talullaah smiled broadly this time.

"Precisely! That was my point!"

"What point?"

"I'm not sure. But … grrrrr … something's going on. I was at first mentioning the likeness my mother has to a fictional character, paying particular homage to the writer … God, what was her bloody name?"

"Whose name?" asked the Muslim, grabbing her latest DKNY bag and proceeding to remove a finger-sized stick of lip-gloss from it.

"The author, who wrote that book. She's really famous. Or was, I'm not too sure."

"What book?"

"That book!"

"I don't know what you're talking about, Maggie."

Sarah groaned. "It's Sarah. My name is Sarah. I don't know why people call me Maggie … well, I partly do. And that book. With Bridget Jones in it. The first was fantastic, but the second was hard to get into."

Talullaah rolled her eyes. "Shut up about your damn books already. I'm sure the 'book' was very interesting. And you only know the pretend reason why you're called Maggie. All that crap about the accident on Open Day last year with the fire and the ambulances and fire engines and police … and calling you Sarah 'Magnesium' Jones. It's just a ploy to assuage you from the main point."

"And what is the main point?" Sarah asked, becoming ever-easily confused.

"I have no idea," her friend replied.

Two

The Marvellous Onus Of Technology

With a calculated sigh, Sarah awaited the weekend, and sure enough, it appeared on Friday afternoon, just as the bell rang to signal end of school. It had been a pointless week, full of learning new things until Sarah had felt that she might stand up and scream for the teachers to shut their great big mouths and stop talking about themselves for a change.

On Friday night, instead of going out, her brother persuaded her to chat with him about his blossoming love-life and what to do with it. "I'm not the one to ask about sex and love," she explained as they stepped into Tony's bedroom. "Out of you and me, who's had the most luck in the love and/or sex stakes?"

Tony shrugged, and sat himself on his dark blue quilt.

"Er, you're the one with the girlfriend. What do I have? Nothing. Faint recollections of almost being raped by that bastard Mr Bates."

"So do I," he mentioned.

"Yeah … but …" She growled. "Stop making things more complicated than they already are. What's your problem? Then I can think about who I can ask to help you." She added with a smile, "You can always ask Mum or Dad."

Tony began to laugh. "You're funny. No, what my problem is, is … well … Hannah." He paused for effect. It had none on his sister.

"Well? What about her? Has she been threatening suicide again?"

He folded his arms. "No. She wouldn't do that to me. Only to her parents. The thing is … her parents." Awkwardly, he crossed his legs, then realised how gay it looked and put them straight again.

"What about her parents?"

"You saw her sister before. Her parents are even worse! Tyrants!" He shuddered. "I had to serve them at the restaurant the other night. Apparently, Mrs Simpson's a house-wife who once was a police officer …"

"Oh, shit …" Sarah ad-libbed.

"Yeah, and her father, Mr Simpson, I don't know what he does, apart from being a right slob … sitting in front of the TV watching it all day. But the scary thing is …"

"What?"

"The TV's been broken for the past three months. And he still watches it."

"I see." Sarah exhaled. "Well, quite a pickle. I know what you have to do."

"What?"

She smiled at him. "Never speak to her parents. And don't invite them to the wedding." He looked hurt, so she continued, "Just … what's the main problem?"

"Er … they won't let me see her as often as I want to. And they especially won't let her stay over here one night … so we could … so I can … we …" He blushed, and attempted to cool down his cheeks by pressing the back of one of his hands to them.

"Don't tell me you're pressurizing her to sleep with you already?"

Sarah stood, leaning against the bedroom wall, and shut her eyes.

"No, not at all."

"That means yes. Tony, you've only been going out with her for about a week or something."

"More like a month."

"A month? Whatever. Still, you can't just shag her after a month."

“Why not?” he asked, becoming a lot more interested after the ‘s’ word was introduced. “People do it all the time. We’re adults.”

“No, you’re not. She’s sixteen, and you’re seventeen. Legal, yes, but you’re not adults. Are you making her feel special by forcing her into sex? No. Girls want romance, love, kisses … proof that her boyfriend cares about her. And don’t go thinking that material possessions don’t work.” She went on, “If you try to win her heart, then maybe - just maybe - you’ll win her heart. I mean, God, what I mean, is that if she falls in love with you, then she’ll want to sleep with you.”

He just raised his eyebrows.

“Were you even listening to me?” she asked her brother.

“Yeah, yeah. So to make her feel special, I have to sleep with her? I get it! That’s what I was trying to do before, but she wouldn’t take the tint. Hint.”

“No, doofus. Make her feel special first.” Irritated at her brother’s stupidity, she said, “You’ll only shag her if you bag her.”

He shook his head slightly. “If that was your attempt to make me remember the facts by giving me a slogan to follow, it’s not going to work. At the most, it sounds like when I took Marie Barker up the arse. You know? In the night-club? When she was wearing that bin-liner?”

“Yes, big brother, I know. I’m going to chat with Jenna now on the Net. Don’t go on the phone. It won’t work. Stupid. Remember last time? You called BT because you thought there were Gremlins down the phone-line, and they couldn’t hear you anyway because of the buzzing and beeping?”

He beamed. “And how’s *your* love-life?”

Sarah's love-life, it seemed, was not as rosy as she didn't make out. And naturally, Sarah's love-life wasn't rosy because she didn't make out. She wasn't a slut, unlike that slag … one of her closest friends, Marie Barker, who had allowed Sarah's own brother to shove something disgusting up something even more disgusting. Her arse.

Her absence of relationship was probably due to the fact that her former headmaster had jumped on top of her and if it weren't due to her slow-thinking, she would have been another victim of the infamous slack-arse and hard, out-of-date stick of salami. Stick of salami? More like a little pink eraser, from what she felt.

Yet she couldn't blame all her faults on Stuart Bates. Her messed-up love-life must have been due to the fucked-up Jones-gene. And why did she have to have such a common surname, anyway?

Sarah moved into the dining room, switched on the light, and turned on the computer. When it had loaded, and the desktop had appeared in front of her worn eyes, she slumped in the white, tattered computer chair which no doubt her mother had had frantic sex on with her lover, Bobby/Billy, and moved the mouse to the Internet logo.

It took two minutes to fully 'blue-bar', and frustrated, Sarah drummed her long thin fingers on the computer table. Soon, she found herself chatting with her closest friend Jenna 'confused hair' Armstrong, on the spontaneous means of conversation called 'messenger'.

The 'conversation', as such, went like this, lasting approximately fifteen minutes: (Starting approximately 2000 hours):

BITHC: *Hi Maggie!*

CHEMSUX: My bloody name is Sarah!!!

BITHC: *Whatever. Hold on. Spelt my name wrong. BRB.*

BITCH: *I'm back. So, what u up2?*

CHEMSUX: Chattin with u, durrr! ☺ Tony's been pissing me off bout Hannah. He wants to shag her & thinks she'll just give in2him if he asks her!

BITCH: *What's wrong with that?*

CHEMSUX: OK, maybe i'm not normal. Maybe I want a bit of romance. How's ur love-life neway?

BITCH: *Hmm ... a bit like ur messenger name. Without the chem. And change the chem4'it'. Tom's here, but he's tossin off over Brad Pitt AND Jennifer Aniston at the same time.*

CHEMSUX: Lol. Why do people call me Maggie?

BITCH: *Cos of the fire, and the Mg, durr!*

CHEMSUX: Is that it? Talullaah was saying the other day it was somethin else, but she didn't know wot.

BITCH: *Oh, you mean about your sister?*

BITCH: *Sarah?*

BITCH: *Sarah? Are u there?*

CHEMSUX: I don't have a sister, unless u mean Tony, but he doesn't look like a boy at all.

CHEMSUX: Girl*

BITCH: *Not Tony. Your twin sister. The one in France.*

BITCH: *Sarah?*

BITCH: *Don't ignore me. It's dead immature if u just ignore me.*

CHEMSUX: I don't have a twin sister. I have a brother. And that's it.

CHEMSUX: Why didn't I know bout her b4 now?

CHEMSUX: If she exists.

CHEMSUX: Which she doesn't.

CHEMSUX: Sarah?

CHEMSUX: Jenna?*

BITCH: *I'm here. I think u shud ask ur mum or dad.*

CHEMSUX: Bithc.

CHEMSUX: Bitch*. ☹

CHEMSUX: ☺ → ☹

End of conversation.

Sarah 'Maggie' Jones hammered on her brother's door. "Tony? Tony!"

"Huh?"

She kicked open the door. Or, at least, she would have done if it hadn't been shut properly. She winced in pain as tingles of agony surged up her leg. She thudded into her brother's room.

"Who's Maggie? I want to know. Tell me everything now, or I'll get a really sharp knife and cut your penis off."

"I'd rather my balls be cut off. They'd hurt more."

"O*kay*. Would you just tell me?"

He exhaled. "Fine. But it's pretty ugly."

Three

Once Upon A Time … & A Non-Chemical Conundrum

"It was a dark and sunny night …"

"What?"

Tony exhaled and folded his legs together, then winced. He extended them again. "Sarah, if you're going to be picky about my descriptions, then don't listen."

"I'm trying *not* to listen," she muttered, and plonked herself next to him on the bed. "But it seems like you're just going to go on and on without giving me a matter-of-fact answer." Sarah glared at him. "I'm sorry. Go on. Woman."

He rolled his eyes and fluttered his dark lashes. "Whatever. It was a dark and windy night, then. And the moon was bright and sparkling, like a torch being reflected on a polished mirror. A girl called Sally, shall we say, was walking in the woods a few miles south of our village, when she happened to hear a tearful, whining cry of a small child. Rushing towards the sound, she felt her heart trip.

"She was aghast when she came across the scene. It was a small child. A baby girl. She had dark, dark hair, almost your colour. In fact, exactly your colour. She had been brought up by grizzly bears in the district who enjoyed drinking the fine nectar the child produced.

"Our young heroine could see that the baby was hungry; I don't know how. Women's intuition or something. Anyway, she reached into her pocket, and gave her a swallow of the mineral water she had. She decided to take the abandoned child home. And when she espied the bottle of water again, the first word that sprung out at her was 'magnesium', one of the minerals that was in the water.

"And so she decided to call the child Maggie. The end."

Sarah breathed breathlessly: "And that child - was - me?"

"No, stupid," her brother replied. "That story was a load of bullshit. Christ, you're so gullible. How the bollocks am I supposed to know who this 'Maggie' is?"

Sarah stormed out and slammed the door behind her.

Two seconds later, she raced into her brother's bedroom again in tears. "Apparently I have a twin sister called Maggie. Who is she, Tony? Who is she, for God's sake? You must know. You're a year older than me, although not wiser and considerably more stupid."

"I dunno. Ask our mother."

"Oh, don't be stupid." She sniffed. "See, demonstrating the stupidity again. You're so stupid it's stupid. How can you be so stupid when there's so many stupid people around who should be a lot stupider than you?"

He grabbed her wrists with his ankles. "Shut up." He stood. "Truth is, I have no blinking idea who Maggie is. Maybe she's a dead twin sister."

She shook her head. "No. Jenna said she's living in France. And I know you're dyslexic, so you won't understand the different tenses. That's present tense. Not past."

"Not understanding tenses has nothing to do with my dyslexia. I'm just thick. And that's what you get from being related to you."

Seeing the bed was free, she threw herself on it and banged her humerus bone, which wasn't amusing at all. She cracked a smile, but only due to the agonizing pain. "Maybe we're not part of this family at all. Maybe we're both adopted. That would make sense, wouldn't it?"

"It would make a lot of sense."

Dr Russell Matthews was having a bit of a problem with his penis.

It was there, he was sure of that, but it was giving him the most terrible trouble. Miss Helen 'Gimme' Moore was also finding his personal pope a bit perplexing, because even though they were sleeping together, they weren't actually *sleeping* together.

He would have assessed it dead, but then again, it kept rising to attention at the most indecent times, such as during lessons when he was standing at the board, trying to explain the male genitals to the first-years. Not that they didn't know what they were, but it was part of the syllabus. Damn it, the syllabus wasn't important! It was his goddamn bacon!

It only seemed to be dead when he looked at Helen. The Languages teacher found it rather offensive, and so she often ignored him in the bedroom and simply fell straight asleep, arms and legs outstretched on *his* bed, almost as if she was waiting for him to pounce on her and stick his rock-hard pork sword into her ... which wasn't going to happen. He could only get it up - to put it crudely - when he didn't think about shafting her.

The male porn he didn't buy helped.

The male porn which, naturally, Talullaah Ali didn't sell to him.

Thinking about his dilemma with his organ of reproductivity (apparently that was what his dick was) in the staff room, and placing a hand protectively over it, he did not notice the ominous shadow cover him.

Only when his sister grabbed him by the shoulders and yanked him up brutally did he pay any attention. It was Monday afternoon, end of school, and the weekend now ceased to exist. Friday moved to Monday in a matter of seventy-two hours, but Saturday and - urgh - Sunday - no longer had names.

"Come on, dipshit. It's time to fly."

He peered up at his sister, hand still over his crotch. She looked at him in dismay. "Oh, jeez. Don't tell me you've been greasing the pipe again. What are you reading there?" She examined the papers that were at the side of him; just a few left-over spot-tests he'd given the fourth-years. "Tests? You were having a fist fuck to *Chemistry?*"

He sighed and didn't even bother responding to Lucy. Had she gained another stone or was it the bad lighting in here? And hadn't he already had that thought, several months ago? Then again, didn't he always think that about the over-weight bully?

"Come on, Lucy. Let's get you home."

"Could you *be* any gayer?"

"What's up her arse?" Tom, cross-dresser extreme, who hadn't actually come out of the closet but got stuck inside it, examining Sarah Jones's backside as she sat on the bus, opposite end to Jenna and her 'boyfriend'.

"Looks like some kind of … stick … like a poker," his alleged girlfriend replied, and kissed him briefly on the lips. He glanced at the window at the back of the bus next to him, catching his reflection.

"Not a bad shade, honey-bunch."

Jenna ignored Tom for a change, and instead made googly eyes at her best friend. Or at least, close friend. Close in that she was sitting a few metres away from her. "Sarah, come on. Talk to me."

"No."

"See, you just talked to me. I'm sorry about Friday. But you've ignored me all day. All weekend, even though Saturday and Sunday have completely vanished off the face of the universe and I couldn't go get my hair done."

Sarah snapped her head around. "You, you, you. It's always about you and your friggin' hair, isn't it? You're obsessed. What about other people's problems, for

God's sake?" She added tautly, "And it's not a poker, it's a metal bar which I'm going to melt and bend for some work in Art."

Jenna bristled. "Well, we've got everything sorted, then. You're obsessed with Art. My problems with my hair don't count."

Sarah rolled her eyes. "Shit, I only want to know the truth about stuff. Why do I always have to go round in circles before I find something out? And then why does it always turn out to be a lie? And then why do I find out that the one thing that I thought was a lie was actually the truth? And I've been living a lie? Eh? Eh?"

Tom looked at Jenna, then Sarah, and shrugged. "It's called Sod's Law. Gee, hon," he said, putting on an American accent and trying to be David Arquette but failing. "If your life was made into a movie, who'd you think'd play you?"

Sarah herself shrugged. "A blonde."

"Sarah, you're a brunette," Tom pointed out. He envied her gorgeous black locks. To say Sarah was apparently a heroine, she had the best hair of them all. According to the theory of Sod's Law that occurred in their lives, because Sarah was the most popular of them all, she ought to have been stunning and naturally have had glossy red hair and pretty blue eyes with a smattering of freckles. Like a comic-book heroine. And neither was she blonde.

"Sarah?"

"Sorry, I was digressing in my mind," she mumbled. "What were you saying?"

"Nothing, nothing," Tom replied.

Four

Revelations

That evening, Marie Barker found herself still at school, poring over some French homework which she'd neglected to do the other day, and was due in tomorrow. It was getting on for seven, and soon the school would be closing. Marie pondered whether she'd get away with sleeping in the common room.

At the moment she was in the main library, but the long-haired Catholic beauty realised she couldn't concentrate in there with all the silence, and so she moved into the her common room, which was situated on the other side of the building.

It was eerily quiet all throughout the school, and slowly she came to terms that she was alone. Marie stepped past the headmaster's study - headmistress's - and spotted that there was a light still on in the study. Surely someone in such high authority as the new head wouldn't stay *this* late after school, would they?

Marie grabbed her French books to her tightly. She inched out a hand and pushed the secretary's door, which was glass, and naturally translucent. Clear, apart from the smudgy fingerprints of perspiring students. Silence.

"Hello? Mrs Jones?" she asked of the headmistress. The headmistress! Who'd have thought that the school would have a female governing the school? It just wasn't thought of! A woman!

"Mrs Jones? Er, Sam?"

Her friend's mother was sitting at the desk, seemingly working. No, no. Not semenly working, seem*ing*ly working. This was not Mr Bates any longer. Mr Bates had had a sex change, a pretty decent one at that.

"Oh, Marie? Hello there. You gave me a fright," Mrs Jones proclaimed. "How are you doing? And what are you doing here so late? It's seven. Have you had anything to eat?"

"No, not yet. Not since lunch-time."

"Well, I've got some sandwiches in my handbag …"

Marie waited for the head to offer her one. The offer didn't come.

"Anyway, Miss Barker. What is it you wanted?"

The dark-haired woman looked up at her student. Marie fixated her eyes on her. Apparently, and Marie hadn't seen proof of this, but eye-contact was a good thing. The headmistress was a pretty thing, obviously taking after her daughter.

"Marie?"

"Oh, um …" She frantically thought of something to say. "I just … wanted to see if you were okay. I mean, in your new job and everything." She smiled, redeeming her sycophantic tendencies. "If there's anything you need help with, I'll always be willing to give you a hand."

Mrs Jones cocked her head. "Now, if you're trying to sell me some drugs, I've already told you I'm not interested."

"No, I'm not."

Sam put a little hand to her mouth. Unfortunately, the hand contained her fountain pen and she managed to endanger her eyes with the nib. Luckily, neither eye was injured in the incident. "Sorry, my dear! I thought you were that Talullaah girl, another of Sarah's friends. Maggie. Sarah. Dearie me, I can't keep up anymore."

"What do you mean?"

Sam Jones smiled slightly. "Now … I know you're Sarah's friend and all, but I can't just tell you this big secret like *that*." There was a pause. "Sit down and I'll tell you everything."

"Don't you think life gets a bit … predictable?"

Sarah's brother peered over at her. "Allegedly, you've found out you have a twin sister who's living in France. How is that predictable?"

They were sitting in the dining room, curtains drawn, playing cards. The light from the bulb hanging above their heads cast a heavy shadow across the table. Tony, dressed in khaki trousers and black T-shirt, glanced over his cards with a smirk.

"Because," Sarah said, picking up a card from the middle of the pile and dropping one again, "I could see something like this coming. My life was going just as imperfectly as possible, just like I wanted it to, and then *this* came along."

He sighed, picked up a seven of hearts, and dropped a Jack. "I know nothing makes sense anymore, but why don't you just try asking mum about it all?"

"That wouldn't work. What she's going to know, apart from everything?"

"No idea. She'll be back shortly. Ask her then."

The telephone rang, cutting their game short temporarily, and Sarah was expected to go pick up the phone, apparently because Tony 'was dyslexic'. She didn't argue the case; there wasn't enough time. It was her mother's lover.

"Hey, Sarah."

"How did you know it was me?" the brunette asked, "I hadn't even spoken yet."

The dark-skinned boy - because let's face it, that's was he was … there was no mistaking his skin colour - chuckled a little. "Just a wild guess. Is your mum there, sweet-cheeks?"

Sweet-cheeks? What on earth?

"No, she's still at work. But it is getting on for eight now. She should be back quite soon." She studied her finger-nails. "Er, Billy?"

"Bobby."

"Yeah, Bobby. Sorry. Habit. Um … do you know anything about my twin sister?"

There was a pause, and for a moment, dialling tone. When Sarah realised that the dialling tone was permanent, she pulled the phone back in shock and came to the conclusion that she must have pressed the green 'hang-up' button with her cheek. Or was she being naïve?

She rang her mother's boyfriend back, just as the woman herself popped through the door with a cheerful 'good evening, children!' and ever-reminding Sarah of the mother in *Flowers in the Attic*.

"Sarah, is that you again?" asked Bobby/Billy. Bobby, dammit.

"Yeah. Sorry, must've cut you off. So …" Sarah moved into the dining room again from the kitchen where she had picked up the portable phone, where her brother was sitting, flicking through the card pile in the middle of the table. Big cheat. "So … what do you know about my twin?"

"She's dead."

"What?"

"According to your mother, she was killed in a horrific mine blast in the outskirts of Lyon a few years back." The twenty-ish guy mentioned, "I have no idea why you don't know about her. Maggie, she was called."

"Maggie. I see. Well, I'd better be going."

"Is your mother there? I know I've just asked, but I heard her tinkling voice a few seconds ago."

"Yeah, I'll just go get her. Hold on."

Sarah passed the phone over to her mother, and then slumped on the dining room chair again. "The game commences. Tony, have you been cheating?"

He just raised an eyebrow.

It was her turn to pick up a card. She picked up a Queen, dropped an Ace, and stated, "Gin Rummy."

The following morning, Hannah Simpson and Sarah were chatting in the common room before lessons. "It must be really weird having your mum being the headmistress."

"She's not really the headmistress," Sarah mentioned. "She's just standing in until the real one comes."

"Okay, if that's what you think."

The dark-haired girl chewed on her lip. "So … how's it going with Tony? And I mean *going*?"

"Sorry, what?"

Sarah stopped chewing her lip, allowing herself to be audible. "I asked how it was going with my brother."

"Oh … fine, fine." She immediately blushed. After glancing around the common room, she finally said, in a conspiring whisper, "Um … I think … he's trying to be romantic."

"What?" Had the cow jumped over the moon? Had dogs started laughing? Had the cat urinated all over the floor? No, that wasn't right at all.

"He bought me flowers."

Sarah growled. "Why can't I get someone like that?"

"You're not looking hard enough. What about … I don't know … Andrew Cage?"

"Puff."

"How do you know?"

"Got long hair. Look at him," Sarah mumbled, and the two girls looked over to the corner of the room, where the dark-haired Andrew was chatting with doing crude things with what looked like Malteasers with his friends. "He doesn't know I'm alive."

"But you like him?"

"Maybe. I haven't considered him … but … um …"

Hannah giggled. "You're blushing, Miss Jones! I can't believe it."

At that second, Marie Barker appeared behind them, and patted them both on the shoulders. "Hey. What you looking at?"

Hmm, to tell her or not to tell her?

"Andrew Cage," Hannah replied, obviously not aware of Marie's tendency to spread rumours and stir the shit as often as possible. The thing was, although Marie had apparently changed, Hannah had had experience of Marie's trouble-making. "Sarah fancies him."

Sarah snorted. "I'd rather fancy my brother. No offence, Hannah. Or Marie."

"None taken," Hannah said. "I don't see why it's offensive. Scary, maybe. But not offensive."

Marie folded her arms. "You know, he is quite cute under that hair. He plays in a band, you know. You know …"

"No, I don't!" Sarah exclaimed. "Why are you American all of a sudden?"

The Catholic was silenced for about three seconds. "Anyway … I happen to know he had quite a crush on the prettiest girl in our year."

Sarah groaned. "Not Talullaah again, for God's sake?"

"No!" Marie answered. "You, stupid."

A small smile found its way onto the raven-haired girl's mouth. "I see."

Five

As If That's Ever A Man's Intentions

"Anyway, we were talking about you and Tony," Marie said to Hannah.

"No," Sarah corrected the Catholic girl, still red from Marie's comment. "*I* was talking with Hannah about Tony. You just walked in two minutes ago."

"Oh. My mistake," Marie answered, and walked off in the direction of Jenna Armstrong and Tom, who were swapping make-up techniques in the further right area of the common room.

"Catholicism," Sarah mentioned. "So … what's the problem about Tony being romantic?" She added, "I must admit," and went a little pink, "it's totally out of the blue. He must really like you. Yeah, I know, he apparently loves you. But you don't know with these skinny lads. Maybe he's just head over heels, smitten with you."

Hannah stated, "I'm worried, though."

"What about?"

"I think that maybe he's wanting to have sex with me, and he's just subconsciously bribing me with flowers and probably chocolates so that soon he'll end up sleeping with me."

Sarah went red again. "Well … God, it's hot in here, isn't it?"

"They've got the radiators off, that's why."

"Oh … okay. Um … well … it's a bit early to be having sex, isn't it? How long have you been going out?"

"A month and a bit. What date is it now? October the something?"

"Yeah, that'll do."

"Yeah, so we've been going out since September … 9th, say. A month and almost two weeks."

Sarah folded her arms. "And he's pressurizing me to have sex with him?"

"No, he's not pressurizing *me* to have sex with him."

"That's what I said. Well, what's your problem then?"

Hannah sighed. "What if he dumps me for not doing it with him?"

"He won't."

"Then fine. We're both acting like adults, even if we're both not yet. I'll go on the Pill. I'll go ask my doctor if I can go on it then." She clasped her hands together. "Oooh, I'm excited now. Maybe I'll do it as a surprise for his birthday."

"His birthday's not until June."

"Well, an early Christmas present."

"Christmas isn't until April."

"Well, I'll do it for Easter then."

The two girls glanced at one another and smiled.

Talullaah Ali found herself in the headmistress's study at lunch time, and self-consciously tucked loose pieces of hair back into her dark blue - not navy - scarf. The Navy was allegedly just for homosexuals, as was all areas of the Armed Forces - even the baby TA. And homosexuality was banned in her house, as it apparently was in the whole of Islam.

Ironically, her brother was a screaming bender - one who liked the 'marmite motorway' and was now dead, and living in Oxford. Oh, how Talullaah loved irony.

Homosexuality … how on earth had she started to think about that subject? Her mind worked in mysterious ways. She had been called into Mrs Jones's study to give a tour around the school for a late-entering student who the headmistress felt especially close to. Hmm. Interesting. Perhaps it was another member of the Krystelle-May gang. And what *was* the black girl's surname, anyway? She'd known her for a month and still not found out. Life's little mysteries. Just like Allah.

When Talullaah finished preening herself, she waited in the headmistress's study, alone, listening ominously to the ticking of the clock and the beat of her thudding heart. For some reason, she always became nervous in areas of authority. Perhaps it was due to the fact that she had several wraps of heroin stashed in her latest furry D&G bag.

Out of the blue, Sarah Jones popped her head around the door, naturally looking for her mother. "Hi," she said to the Muslim girl. "How you doin'?"

Talullaah peered at Sarah, who had scraped her hair back for a change today and was clutching a *darling* little Chloé gold number. My God, had Sarah had a brain transplant?

"I'm fine, thanks. Um … where's your mum? I'm supposed to be conducting a tour."

Sarah shrugged and moved more confidently into the study.

"Have you been borrowing Tony's clothes?" Talullaah asked, studying the outfit Sarah had underneath a smart suit. Gorgeous, truly gorgeous. A lacy blue job from … hmm … French Connection, no doubt.

"No, of course not! Tony?" she asked, inquisitive.

"Yeah, Tony."

"But Tony's male."

"I know," the Muslim girl replied.

"Well, isn't that kind of an insult?"

Talullaah ignored Sarah. "Anyway, when's your mum coming in? I'm starving. I want my dinner, and taking this stupid imbecile around the school isn't really appetizing."

"She told me to meet her here …" Sarah glanced at her silver, designer-label watch. "… round about now."

Footsteps, and in tottered Mrs Jones.

Six

If That Wasn't Confusing Enough For You ...

On Tuesday afternoon, English loomed upon them, and Talullaah and Sarah found themselves sitting in one of Mrs Green's lessons. They had two teachers for English Literature, one of them being a dotty, transsexual, book-throwing false red-head, and Mrs Green. Mrs Green - first name Teresa - was just as bad as the former Mrs Macintosh. Of all the English teachers in the department (four), the two girls had to have the most nutty of them all. Mrs Green had the Christian name Teresa not due to her parents' ironic sense of humour, but in fact it was where she was found after her mother abandoned her. A park, surrounded by several dozen trees. A wood, then.

Mrs Green had closely cropped dark hair, large blue eyes which she hardly ever make-upped due to her stunning plainness, and a 'normal' figure for a woman of forty. She was wonderful to be taught by. It wasn't solely the fact that she was witty, humorous and comic - because she wasn't - but because out of all the teachers in the school, she seemed to *teach* her pupils. Her students gained excellent grades. She was a bitch.

Meanwhile, Talullaah was considerably confused about Sarah's outfit at the moment. Earlier she had been wearing something considerably different. And now, she was wearing a black suit with trousers that didn't match, and had a scruffy old market-job of a bag slung on the floor. Considerably confusing, all right.

"Sarah … er …"

"Yeah?"

"Why did you get changed?"

"Changed?"

Fifty seconds of silence in which Talullaah had chance to further her remarks and answer Sarah's question, and then, apologizing briskly, Mrs Green waltzed in. Actually, it was more of a fox trot. Nevertheless, she threw her books on the desk and sat down. This woman didn't mess around. She was straight down to business.

Mr Miller stood at the front of the lab, one leg cocked up on a stool for pure show. He may be hitting fifty - or had he already? - but he was still supple, if any one had any offers.

Talking of offers, he thought whilst flicking through the dull violet text book in his hands, leaning against his thigh, he wondered whether it was safe now to ask Talullaah for a wrap or two. He'd made quite a bit of money, and now had plenty of useful ways of throwing it away. The method of making the money was probably best left to the imagination: wet lips, wet mouth, wet hand. Sticky hand. Sticky mouth. Sticky belly in some instances. Mouth ulcers. Cash in hand. Mmm … gorgeous smell of money. Heroin. That was the smell of heroin. Oh … no … there was another smell …

"Mr Miller?"

"Huh?"

He shook himself back into consciousness, realising that he had been making noises. He spotted who was talking to him. A lad. Dark hair, long. Christ, couldn't these kids get their hair cut nowadays? He touched his own greying locks with self-consciousness.

"Yes, Andrew?"

"Are you okay? You were making moaning noises. Thought you might be having another heart attack."

Miller touched his paunch slightly, and noticed part of his belly was poking out of his shirt and revealing itself to the class. He moved his hand away and chuckled slightly. "Ha! Ha! No, had enough of those thank you! Ho ho ho!" He cleared his throat, something he seemed to be doing quite often recently. "Now, what are we doing?"

Andrew Cage pulled a face and glanced at his other class-mates who were thinking the same thing: *If he doesn't start teaching us something, I'm going to stick one of his smack needles in his throat!* Harsh, but doable.

At the end of the day, Sarah was cornered by Talullaah Ali in the common room. She didn't know why the Muslim girl had left it until now to ask her such a private question; she'd had all English to probe her, even though Mrs Green had been breathing down their necks due to their lack of concentration on something called a 'Ceremony' in the book they were studying. According to their teacher, if they actually *knew* what this so-called 'Ceremony' was and started paying attention to the text, they might listen and soak in the lurid details. Something to do with fucking, wasn't it? Sarah questioned the teacher. Mrs Green became irate, there was a lot of spittle exchanged, and hair-pulling, and the bells of Hell were also mentioned.

Now, however - digression yet again - Talullaah looked angry. "What are you playing at, Sarah?"

"Huh?"

"And why do you keeping saying 'huh' like it's a real word on our vocabulary?"

"One question at a time, jeez."

Talullaah exhaled. "Why on earth did you get changed after lunch-time? You looked rather swish, even to say it was you."

Sarah narrowed her eyes. "Oh. I was all sweaty. Plus, I didn't think the teachers would let me go around school dressed like that."

"I know," Talullaah said. "What you were wearing must've cost you about six grand."

"Very funny. More like twenty quid." She grinned, and wiped away damp hair. Damp hair? She gave the other girl a wink. "I had quite a work-out at lunch-time."

"With who?"

"Some of the other girls."

"Huh?"

"Talullaah, that word is not in our vocabulary. In netball practice. Why, what were you on about?"

She scratched her forehead, allowing a couple of strands of hair to fall from her scarf. She nibbled at her bottom lip, and then smiled. "Nothing, nothing. Just trying to drive you crazy, Sarah."

“Well, it worked.”

“See you tomorrow.”

After Talullaah had left, Sarah noticed someone sitting at a desk in the corner of the room, poring over some sheets of paper and what looked like a Chemistry text-book, although she couldn’t see anything so it was an educated guess from out of nowhere.

Andrew Cage. Her heart fluttered. She’d heard he was a bender. Better than nothing. “Andrew?”

His head flicked up, and he moved to brush some of his long hair away from his face. Sarah’s mouth went dry. Surely he was making fun at her constant hair-moving? Or was it meant to be? She licked her lips.

“Maggie?”

Oh, bollocks.

Seven

Marie Gets the Shock of a Lifetime & Then Kisses Some Sweet Ass

"It's Sarah, actually."

Andrew Cage had blue eyes. She knew at least that. Sarah Jones was close enough now to spot that her 'crush' was also screwing up his forehead in concentration whilst re-glancing at the book in front of him. Ahh, it was Chemistry.

"Sarah, yeah. You do Chemistry, right?"

"Uh - yeah." Andrew Cage knew she did Chemistry! He knew something about her!

He had thrown off his suit jacket and had his legs crossed under the old rotting wooden and metal desk in the masculine way that some men did. His trousers, a little too short for him, revealed black socks with some yellow cartoon character on them. Sarah wished the trousers would inch up further so she could sneak a look at his legs.

Andrew raced a hand through his hair. "Um, who've you got?"

"Dr Matthews."

"Bloody hell, you're lucky. I've got Mr Miller."

Sarah shuddered. "Poor sod. Has he taught you *anything* this term so far?"

He shrugged. "I have no idea. He mentioned something about a mass spec, and left us to write our own notes. Like we cared. I don't know about you, but …" Andrew Cage sighed. He sighed! It was such a beautiful sound. "… I like to be spoon-fed the work, at least until I know what I'm doing."

Sarah's mouth was so dry now that she found it easy to speak. "Um … well … yeah. What have you … what homework have you got there?"

"Something to do with gas."

"Ideal gas equation?"

"Yeah. God, Sarah, you're smart. I didn't know you were that clever."

She didn't know whether she should thank him for that comment. Still, she drew up a chair and glanced at one of the questions on the sheet of paper Mr Miller had photocopied out of an old textbook. "This is easy. You've got all the stuff provided here, even the number of moles."

"What? Moles?"

She sucked at her teeth. "Okay. Well, first of all, you need to know the equation. PV = nRT …"

Tuesday evening, Hannah Simpson landed on Tony Jones's doorstep with a huge bag on her back. Tony himself answered the door, dressed in an apron and with his hands covered in a mixture of flour, margarine and sugar.

"Are you baking?" were her first words.

"No, no," he replied. "Just messing about. Apparently, if you mix these ingredi-ingrediants together - sugar, flour, something else, and something called fat - and then put it in a funny shaped dish and shove it in the oven, you get a cake."

Pause. "That's baking, Tony."

"Oh. Er … is it raining?"

Hannah looked around her. "No."

"Come in, then."

She screwed her eyes up, knowing that her make-up was ruined and had run down her face. Surely he'd notice? After a few minutes of watching her boyfriend stir the pale yellow mixture, she burst into tears. Obviously, she didn't want to over-act, so she kept the wracking sobs quiet. Tony didn't notice.

She moved up behind him and hit him in the kidney area. "I'm upset, dick-head."

He turned around, a slither of cake mixture in his dark hair. She reached to pull it out. "What's the matter?" he asked, concerned, finally.

"I've run away from home. Can I stay here?"

"Sure," he answered, and turned back to his stirring.

"But you can't tell anyone I'm here, okay? Okay? You can't tell anyone." She grabbed at his sleeve, which was smeared with what she presumed to be dried ejaculation. Or possibly egg. "You won't tell your mother, will you?"

He shook his head, but then swivelled to face his girlfriend again. "How can I not tell her that you're staying here?"

"She's our headmistress. My headmistress, anyway. She'll tell my parents. And I'll get bollocked."

He kissed her forehead. "Hannah, I can keep secrets. But it's going to be remarkably difficult when my mother's living here." He frowned. "It might not work. You might get caught."

"I'll stay with you in your bed."

His face lit up. "Have I told you yet how good I am at keeping secrets?"

Wednesday was the middle of the week, allegedly, and Marie Barker found herself at lunch-time in the I.T. room, chatting to the new technician, Mr Dover. She was immensely attracted to the man, partly because of his bulging package (she was very interested in Microsoft Word and its new facilities) and mainly due to his young age. She guessed he was twenty. She was wrong.

"I'm twenty-three, actually."

"My God. There was I, thinking you were barely out of school." She giggled and touched her cross.

"So what was it you wanted to have help with?" Mr Dover asked, and leaned over Marie as she sat at one of the many computers in the first, larger I.T. room. He was wearing a Calvin Klein aftershave, she knew it. Marie had hung around Talullaah Ali long enough to spot a CK when it was inches away from her.

He had dark brown hair, flicked up in a quiff at the front. He gelled it. It was stiff and suave and sexy, and Marie found herself licking her drying lips as seductively as possible. She looked up at him.

"My - my - um ..." His eyes were an astounding green, and she didn't know why the hell she was glaring into his emerald irises when there was more interesting occurrences. She knew it, without even peering down at his crotch.

For confirmation, she leaned over the back of the chair, where Mr Dover was pressing up. She pushed his body away slightly, to spot a protuberance so obvious that he wouldn't be able to get through the door sideways.

"My ... um ... hard-drive ... at home. Seems not to be working." She slid from the chair and pressed herself against the technician. *Technically*, it wasn't illegal. Then again, technically, neither was it illegal to have an affair with a teacher. But that was just anathema.

Mr Dover smiled a little. "I'll have to help you sort out ... that ... hard-drive."

"Thank-you."

She pushed their mouths together and hungrily kissed him. It was the most pleasurable warmth Marie had felt. She could have done it all afternoon. She reached for his belt but the technician stopped her from loosening it with a swift tap of his heated hands. A few moments later, Mr Dover pulled himself away. His face was flushed and the smile still played on his mouth. "No problem." He walked swiftly out of the room.

Marie had her mouth opened wide, burned by the hot kiss. She found she couldn't speak, and only thoughts plagued her mind as she slumped on one of the computer chairs.

Marie couldn't think for the rest of the afternoon. She found it a hard task in any case, but after the disappointing episode with the Mr Dover, her mind kept revolving back to the point when the I.T. technician raced off as fast as his erection would allow him.

"I got turned down!" she muttered out loud in her German lesson that afternoon, fifteen minutes before the lesson was due to end. Krystelle-May, whose surname hadn't yet been established, was sitting close to her in a semi-circle in one of the Language rooms in the far end of the school.

"Turned down by who?"

Miss Moore, who was busy writing on the board about adjectival endings, swivelled to question what the noise was about. Naturally, it was about someone else's sex life. Miss Moore wasn't having much of one at the moment, and with a sour face, she exclaimed, "Girls!"

“Girls what?” Krystelle-May asked, looking up at the board. “We were just talking about the difficulty in orgasming when you concentrate on it five minutes ago with you. Now what’s the problem?”

“Er, nothing,” the nutty-haired teacher said. She had recently dyed it a darker brown, as if bloody Russell would notice. He never paid any attention to her hair, her appearance, her anything. All he was bothered about was banging away at her as if he were pounding into some kind of animal. “Just … try to concentrate.”

“I thought we weren’t supposed to be concentrating?” Marie asked, looking around the class, allowing for smile to reach her.

“No,” Krystelle-May prodded, “that was about orgasms.”

Marie nodded. “I see. Anyway, someone turned me down. Me!”

“Who?”

The Catholic girl began to blush. “I can’t tell you. I’m going to keep working on him. Let’s just say …”

“Let’s just say nothing, Miss Barker. Start writing these sentences down to translate.”

Marie, curling her long brown hair with her fingers, sat in the headmistress’s office again after school and chatted with her about the problems of life. “I think you should get a dog. You wouldn’t be lonely with a dog in here.”

Mrs Jones sighed. “That doesn’t solve my problem of having twin sisters in my school. Daughters. Whatever.”

“You’re starting to sound like Sarah.”

“Or is it Maggie?”

Marie bit her lip, then said, "So what you're saying is, that your other daughter, Maggie, is in the building?"

"Yes."

"But you don't know who is who?"

"No."

The Catholic girl sucked on her teeth. "That is a bit of a pickle. Why don't you just call them by both names?"

"That's a good idea, which I thought of first." The dark-haired head touched her forehead slightly. "But Maggie has quite a mischievous side to her, which means she's going to make it quite difficult for the lot of us." And then: "And Sarah's just so confused at the moment, people calling her Maggie all the time."

"I can see how it might be a problem."

They smiled together. Mrs Jones continued the conversation: "So what kind of dog do you suggest I get?"

Eight

Conversations Just Aren't What They Used To Be

With every afternoon, there comes an evening, but obviously later and not at the same time. And naturally, if there was an A-bomb dropped on the country that afternoon, the chances of there being an evening would be relatively slim. Nevertheless, on this evening, Hannah Simpson found herself tucked up in Tony's bed - without her boyfriend (who was incidentally in the bathroom not brushing his teeth) - for the second time that week.

They hadn't slept together, but they'd slept together.

When her boyfriend entered the bedroom again, she noticed how he didn't bother switching on the light and yet found the bed in the darkness of mid-October with practised ease. "Hey," he murmurred softly. "Did I snore?"

"You don't snore."

"Don't I?" He raised his brows, without her knowledge, of course. "Well …"

She turned in the bed. "Aren't you even going to ask me why I've run away?"

"It's because your parents are utter bastards and you're so in love with me that you can't stand to spend any less time with me." He took a breath. "And so forth."

"Hmm." After that indescribable word, she continued: "Have you ever heard of the word 'hapless'?"

"Oh, yeah. Means …" There was a gap of silence in which Hannah was positive she could hear the dusty cogs turning inside of Tony's head. "… means … sad, doesn't it?"

She decided not to argue with him. She was too tired to start a conversation. Hold on … hadn't she already?

"Yeah, that's right."

"Woo-hoo!" he said quietly. Moving closer to her until his body was pressing against hers, he inched his mouth closer to hers. "Keep still. I want to kiss you but I always end up missing 'cos you move."

Hannah kept still.

"Darling …"

"Yes Mother?"

Sarah looked up from her quiet smile to eye her mother, who was sitting watching some dire soap opera on the television whilst her daughter ironed the head's clothes for tomorrow. It was getting on for eleven. And when Sarah paid more attention to the soap opera, it seemed more like people taking their clothes off and rubbing up against each other. Jane Austen, then.

"I'm getting a dog for the study. Not for here, mind you. Just for school."

Sarah pulled a puzzled face. "What?"

"A dog. For my office. It gets awfully lonely in there, and your friend Marie suggested it."

Sarah didn't know what to be more confused about; the fact that she and Sam Jones were having a conversation, or that Marie Barker - Marie *Barker!* - was being trusted in such complicated and difficult decisions. She squirmed at both ideas.

"Marie Barker?" Sarah went back to ironing a blue blouse.

"Yes, the young Catholic girl. Very pretty. Innocent as pie. Sleeps around."

Sarah snapped her head up. "What?"

"Ah - but that's just rumours. I hear lots of rumours. Many concerning your specific year, year twelve."

"I know what year I'm in, mother."

Mrs Jones sighed as the break came on, more because of the pause of programming than in what she was about to say: "I do wish you'd come visit me more, Sarah. This morning was nice, yesterday afternoon was even nicer, and Monday … you came twice then. That was splendid."

"What are you talking about? I never came to see you. That would be just too spooky. Really sad, like, oooh, I'm coming to see my mummy, she's the headmistress, nah-nah, so there." She flicked back a piece of hair she was about to iron. "I didn't visit you." She added, "And don't say 'visit', like you're in hospital."

"But -"

"But nothing. And we haven't even discussed the lunacy of the fact that you're bloody headmistress, because I for one don't understand it at all." Sarah continued, irate, feeling steam pour out of her ears and then realising that she had the iron too close to her face, "But no one seems to give a damn about lunacy around here. It's like that book … I can't remember what it's called … anyway … that's not the point."

"But it is."

"Whatever."

"Ah! That's what Marie was talking about!"

Sarah growled. "I don't understand why everyone else knows everything around here apart from me."

"Probably because you're your father's daughter, and everyone else isn't." Mrs Jones went on, "Apart from Andrew, of course."

"Tony. His name is Tony." Sarah had the distinct feeling that this conversation wasn't getting anywhere. "If you don't tell me what's going on soon, then I'm - I'm going to go to *someone else*."

Before Sarah's mother could reply, however, the living room door swung open, and a pink-faced Tony entered. Pink, possibly because he had a smearing of blood on his face which he had tried to wash off.

"Mum, Sarah, do you have any … um … er … tampons? Or … um … pads?"

Sam Jones burrowed her brows. “Why, Andrew?”

“Experiment,” he answered quickly.

“In my top cupboard.”

Tony left the room, his sister shortly following. “Why didn’t you just ask me? It’s for Hannah, isn’t it?”

“No, I’m doing an experiment.”

“Liar.”

“True.”

They smiled. “Anyway, why didn’t you ask me?” Sarah questioned. “How long do you think Hannah’s going to be able to stay here undetected?”

“I figured about … hmm … two years, so she can finish her studies at high school, and then we can move away to whichever university she wants to go to.”

She smacked her forehead, and was grateful that she’d left the iron in the living room. That could’ve been a painful accident. “Tony, are you crazy?”

He shrugged. “Probably.”

“I’m sorry, I don’t know what happened,” Russell mumbled to his bed partner, the elusive Helen Moore. “I’m tired.”

Her Majesty frowned. “I understand.”

She rolled over in bed and fell asleep as soon as her heavy breathing and racing pulse regained their normal rhythms. Russ Matthews lay awake all night, not being able to comprehend why his rocket, which he so often polished in the school grounds now, was not up to business.

Nine

Apparently The Weekend & Marie Gets Her Cum-uppence

"It's Thursday already," sighed Krystelle-May as she sat with Lucy Matthews in the library, "the weekend already."

They both were helping the librarian wrongly number the books in the Dewey Decimal system, due to the fact that they were both on detention for 'uncouth behaviour', as Mrs Jones politely put it.

Lucy twitched her podgy nose, then arched a brow. "There's Friday first."

"Friday?" the black girl asked, who was about the same height and weight as the school bully, "What's that?"

Lucy scratched at her bleached blonde hair which was turning brown with peroxide deficiency, then found herself smiling as they waited for the librarian - neither man nor woman - to lug a heavy box of new school books into the main library area. Lucy slumped on the desk, where many students would have been trying to get books out if it weren't for her fat arse.

"Anyway," Krystelle-May smirked, "what's it like having a puff of a teacher as a brother?"

They were in competition. Lucy could see it the new girl's eyes; the reason they were in here in the first place was almost a competition in itself. Krystelle-May just beat her; the darker girl had two fists full of hair whereas the plump pig had only one. Oh, and it made Lucy so pissed off.

"I don't know what it's like. What's it like killing several people?"

"I didn't kill them. My psychotherapist says that they were just unfortunate accidents."

"My psychotherapist says there are no such things as unfortunate accidents."

Krystelle-May swallowed. "Oh."

"So … end of conversation. And don't think you've got the slightest chance of becoming the new school bully - or even another one - because I'm the one and only. I won't stand for any shit." Lucy narrowed her pudgy eyes. "I know you won me last time, but that was pure fluke."

Krystelle-May smiled. "I understand, Lucy."

The dog arrived earlier than either Marie or Mrs Jones had anticipated. It came in a cardboard box on the Thursday afternoon at around four, wrapped in a pink ribbon with the words: FRAGGILE: GOD IN BOCKS.

Sam Jones sucked at her bottom lip in a way that Marie had often seen her daughter do, then tapped her foot on the polished floor without effort. Or so it seemed. "Hmm."

"Yes, Mrs Jones?"

"Should I open it now, or wait until the morning when I'm fresh as a daisy?" the headmistress asked, studying the double-sellotaped sealed box with anxiety. "I think I might bung it next to the fire and open it tomorrow with the post. It can be a surprise!"

Marie wrenched out a little morality from that Catholic religion of hers. "But Mrs Jones!" That was it. A little.

"Yes, Marie?"

"The dog."

"Yes."

"It's inside the box."

"Yes."

"Won't it suffocate?"

Mrs Jones laughed, tossing back her jet black hair. "Don't be silly, dearie. The dog I ordered from the catalogue is a Labrador. A clever dog. Surely it can survive in a fragile little box, can't it?"

"It wasn't ordered from - well - um - of course, what ever you say, Mrs Jones."

"Good, good. Now, let's be off. I have to go home and not make the children's teas."

They started to move out of the study, with Marie jerking her head back several times to where the box containing the dog was sitting. "Er - Mrs Jones …"

"Yes, Marie?"

"I think I left my jacket in there. I'll sort out the lights and everything."

"But you're wearing your jacket."

"My bag? No, I definitely left my bag in there."

Mrs Jones screwed up her eyes. "I could swear you just said you'd left your jacket in there."

"That's what an eight-hour work-day does to you, Mrs Jones. Don't worry, I'll sort out everything."

The headmistress beamed, and reached out for Marie's cheek. "Thank you ever so much, Marie. I'll make sure you're rewarded in the long-run. I think I could do with a head-girl to look after me. You seem like the perfect candidate."

"What's -"

"Oh, something we used to have at the school where I went to," the head replied. "Donkeys' years ago. And that's donkey after donkey after donkey." She smiled. "Thank you, Marie."

After the clipping of heels disappeared into the distance, Marie rushed into the study and snatched a letter opener from the desk organiser on Mrs Jones' lavishly polished work table. She slit open the box with haste, and slowly and uncautiously unflapped the cardboard … flaps. A puppy stared up at her, mournful. "Hello."

He didn't answer, no doubt sulking from being cooped up in the box for so long. Marie reached in with long slim arms to lift the puppy out of the 'bocks', when the telephone rang.

She answered it. "Hello?"

"Mum … I'm sick of staying at this hotel … can't I come home?"

Marie pondered her options.

She hung up.

Just as Marie Barker was rushing out of the study, switching off the lights and slamming the door shut, she heard a fairly masculine voice behind her, which shook her so tremendously that she didn't feel the rough hands on her shoulders.

Mr Dover, the I.T. technician. "Miss Barker … what are you doing in there?"

"I'm …"

Indeed, what was she doing? Naturally, she lied. "Nothing." Marie quickly figured out that what she'd said was the truth after all, so she decided to concoct a web of lies. "I was helping Mrs Jones lock up. I told her I'd switch off the lights and everything." Another bout of truthfulness. What was going on? Why did she feel the need to tell the ugly truth to someone as handsome as the oak panelling?

"I see. And what's that … that … god awful smell?"

"The dog."

"Dog?"

"Yes. Mrs Jones has bought a dog to keep her company because of the loneliness she suffers in this empty school."

Mr Dover looked confused. "There are close to a thousand students in the school at any one time. How is that empty?"

Marie pulled away from his grasp and murmurred. "Anyway … I have to go. Have to … go …"

"Marie?"

She stumbled out of the secretary's area of the study, and down the dark corridors which were blazing with the thick glow of light.

"Marie? Miss Barker?"

She turned on her heels, almost skidding to a halt on the shiny, newly unpolished floor, and cocked her head. "What?" She added, almost remembering again after totally forgetting that he was a teacher: "Sir?"

"Drop the cute act, Marie. Everyone in the school knows what a slut you are. Sleeping around with anything with breasts." He continued, "And women too."

Anyone else would be insulted, but with anyone else, it wouldn't be true. "And your point is?"

"Do you fancy a quickie?"

Marie's eyes lit up. "Thought you'd never ask." She moved towards the head's study again and the two of them took their time christening each piece of furniture in the room … and then they proceeded in the sex-having.

Ten

The Aftermath

Sarah's relationship with Andrew Cage had yet to develop in such a rapid manner as her fellow friend's and the I.T. technician, but Sarah found herself teaching Andrew during almost every lunch-time, and Friday was no exception, apart from the fact that it hadn't happened yet.

At around elevenish - all the clocks were wrong; apparently it was something to do with appreciation on Kafka - Andrew walked up to Sarah and gave her a goofy grin. His long hair was still long, yet it looked like he'd used conditioner for a change. She could smell Herbal Essence or Avon's own brand - who could tell the difference? "Hey, Chem buddy!"

He always called her that, and no matter how many times Sarah poked him and prodded him and allowed her hand to rest on his thigh whilst she told him not to call her it … he still did. She reckoned he might be a bit thick. Then again, he was doing Chemistry for a sixth-form subject. Not that that meant anything.

"Hi, Andrew."

"It's Andy."

"And I'm Sarah."

"I know."

They stood in silence for a moment, considering the fact that they only had about ten minutes before morning break ended and they'd have to scoot to the next lessons, which didn't actually exist for either of them for several reasons: both Sarah and Andrew were skipping English and Maths respectively.

"Is the date still on?" Andrew asked her, tossing back a lock of his gorgeous yet horribly long hair. Laziness. Pure laziness. She'd never go out with him, not with his hair as long as it was now.

"A date? When? Where? What time? With me? I didn't … um … oh, God, what will I wear? Um …" Sarah flustered a little with her hair, mirroring Andrew considerably.

"I mean you teaching me Chemistry this lunch-time."

Sarah stopped moving mid-fluster. "Um … I know. I was just joking. *Our* library?" she asked with a little giggle which she purposely made sound blonde.

"Okay. One?"

"Sure."

And that was that. Was she so fantastically brilliant at Chemistry that he needed her to teach him it every single lunch-time? Or was he finding any excuse -

but the same one each day - to spend time with her? She hoped it was the latter. She had such a huge crush on him now. Not thinking about him when she went to bed wasn't even an option anymore.

She sighed and grabbed her bag so she could go pretend to be sick in the toilet and land herself in the sickroom, wanting to avoid Mrs Green. Punishment for not doing her homework was equal to a good whipping, naked and in front of the whole school, Andrew Cage in the front row.

Lunch-time couldn't come any sooner.

Marie Barker pattered into the headmistress's study that lunch-time to find a unholy mess. It looked like Mrs Jones had had a wild party and not invited her; tearing up the large maroon drapes by the windows and rolling up in them, shitting on the carpet in what could only be described as a green, 'trot'-like manner, and chewing into the multiple-thousand pound desk. Then Marie realised that she had been the last one in the study … with Mr Dover.

Going pink not with embarrassment but humiliation because she had stepped in a pool of what she could only hope was saliva, Marie exhaled, "Mrs Jones! --- What happened?"

It took Marie fifteen seconds to notice that Mrs Jones wasn't in the study at all, but standing out of earshot in the secretary's quarter. She trampled into that area. "Mrs Jones … what happened in there? It looks like World War Three all over again."

Mrs Jones, today wearing a timeless black pinstripe suit - just as she wore every day - flicked at her ebony hair. "More like World War Four. Have you seen all the excrement?"

Marie simply nodded.

"The little *merde tête* - excuse my German - French - *Scheisskopf* -" Mrs Jones was blustering about, naturally not wanting to look back in her office. "- He must have escaped and caused havoc. Heaven knows how the little rascal jumped onto my desk, though, and allowed all the papers stacked neatly in files to be sprewn all over the floor. Goodness, is sprewn actually a word? Apparently not." Mrs Jones inhaled deeply. "*Scheisskopf* really … more like *Scheissarsch.* Excuse my bad language." She shook her head vigourously. "And he even …" Mrs Jones looked like she was about to tell a dirty joke, apart from the fact that her face was deadly serious. "Well, you're a big girl now, Marie. I'm sure you're old enough to … understand. The little rascal … *humped* on the sofa … *and* the *desk*, *my* desk! and left his … juices after him. You'd have thought he'd have had the gumption, the audacity, to lick his fluids up after him, wouldn't you?"

Marie shrugged. "I … I don't know. Where … where is he now?"

"Asleep, wrapped in one of the curtains. Oh, dear me, Marie. How am I going to sort out all this *mess?*" She peered at the Catholic girl hopefully. Marie smiled broadly.

Bollocks to German.

Eleven

Will He Ever Just Go Away?

"So what are the plans for tonight then?" asked a pepped Richard - Dickhead as his fellow colleagues fondly called him - Burch.

Dr Matthews, scratching his head simply because it was habit, frowned and grinned at the same time. "Sorry, mate. Not going out this week. It's not pay-day yet."

Burch, the Psychology student teacher who seemed constantly to stay in a position of low authority and appeared to be happy about it, rubbed his hands together. "Bet you can't wait 'til flippin' next Friday, eh?"

"Hmm," replied Mr Miller for his fellow Chemistry teacher.

It was lunch, and Dr Matthews was poring through a copy of a highly publicized, highly criticized and highly priced magazine which most of the house-wives in Britain who hadn't killed themselves with bleach poisoning read. It was one of those glossy, plastered with photos magazines which revealed how one celebrity was splitting up with one celebrity; one celebrity had a drug-habit which - bless them - they were trying to keep underwraps so they could eventually die of an overdose just before going into rehab; and how one celebrity liked it anal-style. Yum. The readers were forced to believe the faeces that was printed in the publications simply because they cost almost ten times as much as a tabloid.

Dr Matthews hadn't just found the magazine, which shall remain nameless due to legal reasons, on the coffee table in the staff-room. Oh, no. On the afore mentioned table lay copies of *Angler's Edition, Trains 'R' Us, Pornstars: What You Didn't See on Sky Digital*, and so forth. The Chemistry teacher wasn't fussed about those sorts of things.

He'd snuck into the local shop earlier this lunch break - bumping into Maggie Jones as he went. Apparently, she was amused and bemused - dammit, it *is* easy to confuse those words! - that her teacher (even though he didn't teach her) was buying such a pansy publication. He'd dropped it next to a music magazine on the side, and asked for a packet of fags, despite never smoking a cigarette in his life before.

"Er … Maggie …" he had stuttered fifteen minutes previous to now, "…er … you'd best not say anything about this."

The jet-haired vixen - vixen? - had grinned, walked out of the shop, and left him to shame-facedly pick up the magazine again and pay for it. When he'd stepped out into the rainy sunshine, the head's daughter was standing there waiting for him.

"You teach at the school, don't you?"

"What? How do you know that?" Russ was becoming increasingly confused as the seconds bore on. "Hold on - Sarah - I teach you."

"No, I'm Maggie."

"No, you're Sarah."

"I'm Maggie. You just called me Maggie."

"But I always call you Maggie, 'cos of the magnesium business. And don't start fighting about that again. Yes, I knocked over the Bunsen burner, but you were the one who poured the whole grey, cylindrical bottle - without lid - into the device."

Maggie had looked confused. "I'm Maggie. I know it's confusing. Not even Sarah knows I'm here."

"Huh?"

"I'm … God … it's too difficult to explain to someone with such great intelligence as yourself. One day, hopefully, everything will be out in the open."

Russ had shook his head. "You're Sarah. How can you be someone else, if you're Sarah?"

"I'm Maggie Jones. I'm her sister!"

Dr Matthews felt like smoking. He bit at a nail instead. "How can you be her sister? You're identical!"

The dark-haired girl groaned. She glanced at his pass, which was dangling from his suit jacket. "Dr Matthews. The infamous. Interesting." With that, she stalked off, down the street, away from the school.

"School's this way, Miss Jones!"

She had ignored him.

Now, in the staff-room, it wasn't just the fact that he was recalling the incident twenty minutes ago as if it was happening in the present moment that pissed him off, but that the magazine pages were sticking to his perspiring fingers. He glanced up.

Richard 'silent H' Burch was still standing over him.

"Would you just piss off?"

Sarah was sitting in the library, peering at Andrew Cage's gorgeously smooth skin and the gorgeously gorgeous stubble which he had let grow, much to the ignorance of the staff. His eyes were gorgeous. They had these, these … well, almost like eyelashes. And brows. Sarah reached out, daring herself to touch one of his eyebrows - generally the one which was nearest to her. Instead, she pretended to be placing her hand on the sheet of paper Andrew was writing on to check his answer to the practice questions he was attempting.

Suddenly, out of nowhere apart from next to her, he looked up, cricked his neck, then looked down again. Hand on neck, he blushed. Perhaps it was the pain from pulling the muscle. Andrew mumbled something.

She didn't hear him, so presumed he was asking whether he'd got the question right he was trying to do. "Hold on, I'll just look in the back of the book," she said, lifting up the text book he was working from and leafing to the last few pages.

"I said, Should I get my hair cut?"

Sarah almost turned the colour of the text-book, which quite unfortunately was purple and green with white stripes. Instead, she managed a maroon colour which was as close to the purple as she could get. "Um, er, um, I …"

He'd asked a question which men hated to answer. Sarah wondered whether she should have a sex-change, as she was finding it awfully hard to answer it herself. Then again, she had to consider the question put to her. She'd always wondered what he'd do with his long hair when they went to bed. Would he let it smoothly lay loose, lying on her as he pumped inside her? Perhaps she would go on top to return the favour. She could feel the shoulder-length black, hair-like gold run over her body and she shivered. Or maybe it was a wig, and he was testing her. Maybe a detachable device. She went pink, now. A safe colour, yet still looked like she was choking.

"Um … why not?"

"Well, that's what I thought. Seeing's that it's Summer now, nice and hot."

"Andrew, it's October the nineteenth."

"Oh, yeah. Right. I knew that."

Dr Matthews flung down his copy of the magazine after scouring for hot male celebrities - purely to check the fashion sense - and looked over his shoulder again, Richard 'silent H' Burch was still standing there. Strangely, Dr Matthews was sure he'd seen the man leave.

"Yes?"

Richard folded his arms. "What are you so interested in those glossy pages for? I thought those pages were only for mid-wives."

"House-wives, Richard, and no. Not just house-workers are - oh, would you just fuck off, for God's sake?"

Richard failed to see the irritation blazened across the teacher's face. "Ooh, we are waving the obscenity stick around, aren't we? What's the matter, Russell? Had another boo-boo in the lab? Sarah Jones getting to you again?" The student-teacher smirked. "No-one will be surprised when you come out, Shirley."

Russell creased up his eyes, solely because of the light of the staff-room windows piercing his pupils. "What are you talking about?"

"Heaven's above! You're about as camp as that camp fellow on the telly. What's he called? The chat-show host?"

"Graham Norton?" he offered.

"No, no. Richard Madeley. By God, is he singing the wrong National Anthem!"

Dr Matthews rose, prepared to knock the Psychology student-teacher across the room with someone else's fist, and then instead turned to Mr Miller, who still sitting next to him. Well, not technically. Russell was standing, Iain was sitting. Still, same thing, yet not.

"Mr Miller. A word."

"Yes, Dr Matthews."

"Outside."

"Right."

The two of them left the staff-room to the ever-brightness of the dull corridors. A few students were standing outside, waiting for staff to exit the communal room so that they could mace them.

"Dr Matthews! Dr Matthews! You've got to help us!"

Ah, to be not popular. First-years. Brilliant.

"Yes, Joanne? Julie? Jane?"

The three girls looked at each other excitedly and in fear. "There's this great big green thing in our form-room! Huge!"

"Yeah!" screamed another girl. "Massive!"

"Yeah, come help! We think it might've escaped from the biology lab! It's, like, five metres long."

Dr Matthews turned to his fellow teacher and measured with his hands. They didn't make five metres. He sighed. "Girls, are you sure this thing is alive?"

"Yeah," the tallest one said, "it's moving and stuff. It's so big!"

Mr Miller leaned towards Russell, and said quietly, "Who do we call about something like this? The fire brigade?"

Dr Matthews whispered back, "Environmental agency ideally, but with a situation like this, we might not have enough time."

"It's not certain the emergency services will turn up in time."

"Just call them anyway. All we need is for this thing to go around and eat a few people."

Mr Miller nodded. "I'll call them. You go see if you can prise into the room. Something like this, it could've morphed and multiplied in size within minutes. And Dr Matthews," he said, raising his voice, "be careful."

Dr Matthews saluted and headed with the three girls towards their form-room.

Twelve

I Think The Right Phrase Is 'Bollocks!'

Room twenty was up a flight of stairs, along a long corridor and took them five minutes to get there. Still, those five minutes lasted a life-time. Russell felt his mouth go dry and his insides curl up as if admitting defeat. He'd never felt so much like a soldier.

He inched open the door, expecting it not to open. He could hear voices, giggles, and the occasional girly-squeak. He swallowed. There were possible casualties in the room. Russell inhaled and stepped into the room.

Several pupils were crowded around something on the teacher's desk which wasn't five metres long.

"Get back, everyone. Back! Let me through!"" he shouted. When a gap finally formed, he was dumb-struck by what he saw, yet somehow found the words to speak. "Girls … that's a caterpillar."

"What did the fireman say?" Russell asked, staring blankly out of the window in room twenty, which was covered in foam.

“It’ll cost you a couple of grand.”

Mr Miller leaned against the wall, trying to find a patch that wasn’t spread with the white gooey stuff. “Sorry, mate.”

“A couple of grand? I haven’t got a couple of grand! Well, I have, but who’s to know that? Ah, charge it to Mrs Jones.” He exhaled, and peered around the room. Whiteness. White, white, white. Apart from the floor, which was soaked in water and displayed warning boards, everywhere was covered in foam.

“It’s the foam that costs so much, Russ. They thought they were dealing with a six foot monster. They brought several gallons of the stuff. Which is why it’s all in this room.”

“All over a bloody two-inch caterpillar. God, I’m going to lose my job over this, aren’t I?”

“Yeah, probably.”

Dr Matthews opened his eyes wide. “You’re supposed to support me and say no! And -” He turned his head. “Can you shut that lot up out there? It sounds like a riot out there.”

“It is. All the first-years want to come in and have a look. They’re all down the corridor.” Mr Miller sighed. “Come on, it’s not that bad. Just think, when you lose your job here, at least you won’t see Sarah Jones again.”

The teacher folded his arms, and found a piece of foam on his sleeve which he brushed off, irritably. “Why do people think I have such a problem with her?”

“’Cos you’re always complaining about her.”

“Well … oh, yeah! That’s what I wanted to talk to you about, before. I saw Sarah down at the shop earlier, and she claimed to be someone else.”

“She’s always doing that. Did that to me yesterday.”

"She said she was called Maggie."

Mr Miller scratched the top of his nose. "Hmm. Playing our game now, is she? Trying to confuse us?"

Russ shook his head. "I don't think so. She said she was Sarah's twin sister, Maggie, and that she was staying here. I don't recall Mrs Jones saying anything about that in the staff-meeting this morning, or last week."

"Yes - she did. Weren't you listening?"

"No. Were you?"

"Does anyone?" Mr Miller admitted. "Richard Burch was listening, though."

"Oh, typical."

"I know. He said that Maggie, Sarah's twin, of whom Sarah didn't know existed, is back in Britain after living in France most of her life. And that Maggie has a different father to Sarah."

Dr Matthews raised his bushy brows. "How does that work out?"

"It doesn't. That's something I made up to see if you were listening." He continued, "Anyway, why is it any of our business? You're got bigger problems." Mr Miller swept a hand across the expanse of the room. "You'd best try get this stuff sorted out."

"Mrs Jones ... could I please have a word? It's about your dog." Dr Matthews inched himself quickly into the headmistress' study and popped his head around the room. She was in there, he knew it, because he couldn't see her.

"My darling puppy? I hope he hasn't been doing any more whoopsees on the hall-way walls again!" Her voice came from behind the sofa, which was adjacent to the right hand wall, next to a large spider plant and a great big cupboard full of wine glasses and the like.

"Mrs Jones? Where are you?"

"Next to the sofa."

Dr Matthews moved around the leather item of furniture, and wondered whether she'd done the dirty on it yet with her boyfriend, or affairee, Bobby. Or was it Billy? All he knew was that he was teaching Krystelle-May, his sister. He found the head scrubbing at the side of the couch with a scratty old cloth which it looked like she'd just bought.

"What are you doing?"

"The blooming dog. Haven't got a name for her yet. He's a right little fuss-bucket. Got all his stuff on the sofa."

"Stuff? And is it a boy or girl?"

"Undecided."

"I see." He cleared his throat. "Mrs Jones …"

"Sam."

"Yes, I know. Mrs Jones, if this is a puppy … a recently born one … what do you mean by stuff, anyway? I might have totally misunderstood you."

Sam Jones creaked to her feet and brushed her dark skirt down with her manicured nails which a snob would be proud of. I mean, aristocrat. She tossed her hair from side to side. "Ejaculation, Russell."

He bit his lip. Then, after trying to speak but finding he couldn't, released it from his top teeth. "Um … have you ever had a dog before?"

"No … well, yes."

"Huh?"

"Well, we thought it was a dog, and it turned out to be a hamster. Little thing, it was. Gorgeous. Had it when I was ten. After the war. Beautiful. Furry."

Russell raised a brow. "Mrs Jones, you're forty-three."

"I know. After the war. 19-whatever." She bent her back to peer at the stain again, which had dried what she described as 'yuckily'. "Look at it … it won't come off."

"Mrs Jones," the Chemistry teacher remarked, "that can't be the dog's semen. He's not old enough. It's human … semen." He felt like a little kid in high school again, and blushed furiously. He was determined to be on the right side of authority for a change.

"Human? Well … who's been in here then? It's not mine," she answered.

Russell wondered whether she realised what she had just said.

"Hmm," was all he replied. "Then it must be someone else's." He exhaled. "Anyway, I came to speak to you about something else."

"I thought you said you wanted to speak to me about my doggy?"

"I did," he lied. "But there's something else. Your daughters."

Mrs Jones swallowed thinly. "I see. You'd better … not sit down. Here. Er … over by the desk."

A little while later, Russell had the whole story. It was a lot fuzzier than earlier. He had folded his legs like the woman that he was and left his fingers lying on the table in front of him.

"So, what you're telling me is that Sarah has a twin sister who is *dead*, who's living in a hotel locally?"

"Um … yes."

Russell thought of himself as intelligent, although that wasn't actually proven. And he was bloody confused. "That doesn't make sense."

"Nothing does, Dr Matthews. What I mean is," Mrs Jones mentioned as she flicked back a lock of ebony hair, "her sister is meant to be dead. But she's not. She's been living in France since she was six."

"And she's called Maggie? I don't understand. Then why am I calling her Maggie all the time? Solely because of Sarah's accident with magnesium? Isn't that slightly coincidental?"

Sam Jones nodded. "That's it. For eleven years, Maggie has been but a *blip* in Sarah's life. I've tried to introduce her back into the school slowly, but apparently she hasn't been sticking to the rules of our 'agreement' as tightly as she should have been."

"Agreement?"

"Don't turn up at school. At all. Unless I say so."

Before she could continue, Russell reached out a dangerous hand - the dangerous hand, which he'd spilt bromine on the term before - to block out Mrs Jones's face. "As much as I admire you, and fancy your pants, Mrs Jones, what I'd like to know is why in the first place you gave away Maggie's twin sister. Sarah's."

"It's a long story. I can't remember."

Thirteen

When Will They Learn That Girls Don't Need Sport?

"Oh, I see." Dr Matthews scratched his forehead, then said, "Anyway, there's something more dangerous to worry about, anyway. Um …"

"Dr Matthews - are you -" The head silenced herself for a second. "-are you *repeating yourself*?"

"Um … yes. There's a slight problem down in one of the language classrooms. It occurred this lunch-time. And was almost entirely my fault. But not. The sirens you heard earlier …"

"Yes, I know about them."

The Chemistry teacher inhaled sharply, and expected to be beaten. He wasn't looking forward to it; probably because Mrs Jones was a woman. He believed.

"You *do*?"

"Yes. Mr Miller told me. It was some great big biological mutant that had escaped from the Biology lab. Biological error, I presume. Biology, biology, biology. Ban it, I say. No use in it."

"Of course."

"You did it to A-level, didn't you?"

"Er, yes."

"So really, you enjoy Biology, don't you, Dr Matthews?"

"Er, yes."

She sighed. "You should really learn to gain some confidence when you're around your boss. Not that I believe that I have any greater authority than you, which I do, but nevertheless, I want us all to get along swimmingly." She nodded to herself. "I know what you've had to go through with that -" She lowered her voice. "-*bastard* Mr Bates, but consider it this way: if you feel you ought to be scared of me, then do so. But if not, then treat me like the equal that I'm not." She clapped her hands together. "Now, this mutant thing. It's going to be cleaned up, isn't it?"

"Yes, Mrs Jones, it is."

"Good. Then you're dismissed."

She caught his expression. "That was a joke, Dr Matthews."

"Of course, of course." He stumbled to his feet. "I'll be going. Good luck with that man-stain."

"Man-stain? Ah, the semen." Mrs Jones smiled and folded her arms at her desk. "Naturally. I'll find out the rascal who defecated in my office."

Russell raised his eyebrows. "He shat in your office too?"

Flustered, Mrs Jones looked around the room. "Er, you're dismissed, Dr Matthews." When he shut the door quietly after himself, the headmistress pulled out a small notebook: *Defecation; to excrete bodily waste.* "Really, Sam, you should have known that."

Sworn enemies Krystelle-May and Hannah Simpson had one thing in common: they hated each other's guts. And the rest of each other. So when Hannah found herself paired up with the large black girl, Lucy Matthews and Jenna Armstrong trailing behind in their 'group' for the Games lesson, it was like Night of the Living Dead.

They were orienteering. And it wasn't funny. In fact, it was bloody hilarious, and Hannah found herself laughing despite the irony of whom she had been joined up with.

“Who picked these groups?” Jenna was muttering to herself, plucking hopelessly at her short nut-coloured hair. “And why am I even here? It’s not like I’m of any importance. No one needs me. I’m just a girl with funny-coloured hair.”

Hannah stopped, dressed in the stereotypical white-striped black jogging bottoms and a large, thin blue sweater. She turned to face Sarah’s best friend. “You’re here to help spot the things that we’re supposed to be finding. And to stop me committing suicide.”

“Hmmph,” Krystelle-May mumbled. “That should be difficult.”

Lucy sniggered, her bleached hair yanked back from her head. Yanked back, because Jenna Armstrong had the school bully by her podgy pig-tail - this time, not the one sticking out of her arse.

“You just shut the fuck up, would you?”

Lucy snarled, and Jenna pulled harder.

“Take your ammonia-stained hands off of me.”

Jenna pulled tighter. “I only use recommended hair-dyes which are not permanent, and therefore do not contain enough ammonia to stain my hands.”

“Bollocks. My brother’s a fucking Chemistry teacher. Ask him about it.”

Sarah’s best friend dug her fingers in Lucy’s scalp. Lucy made a snorting sound. “Ask him how to stain my hands? Yes, he’s very bloody good at doing that. Bromine, iodine, ammonia, magnesium … you name it, he’s spilt it in our lessons. Had lithium flying up at us.”

She sniffed. “He can’t help … the reactivity … of the elements. Lithium is only so reactive because it has an outer electron that needs to escape from the outer shell.”

“Oh, bollocks to you,” Jenna snapped, and tightened her grip.

Hannah tried to call the peace, whereas Krystelle-May was enjoying herself and attempted to thump her former friend out of the way so she could watch the fist-hair fight.

"This isn't getting us anywhere," Hannah murmurred. "Let's just try and cheat as quickly as possible. Jenna, do you remember where all the signs were from year-eleven?"

Jenna released Lucy finally, much to the bully's relief. Lucy touched her sore head delicately. "I wish you wouldn't hurt me there. You know it's my second-best feature." As if to cave in even further, she reached into her stereotypical striped bottoms and pulled out a sheet of paper. "Here's all the answers. Who's up for a drink at the pub?"

Jenna and Hannah glanced at one another.

Fourteen

David: The Joke Won't Be Appreciated By Many

At the end of school, Sarah was called into her mother's office by Mrs Macintosh, who incidentally wasn't named after a computer. For then she would be called

Macintosh Macintosh. "Sarah, love, your mother wants you," proclaimed the red-haired English teacher, who had also managed a sentence without stuttering.

Sarah had been walking towards the staff-room to hand in some English homework for Mrs Green a day late (and was dreading the hair-tearing and shrieking when the lesson occurred on Monday), when the transsexual exited the staff-room and made a slapping noise against her cheek with a very female hand. Her own, naturally.

When the headmistress's daughter popped into the study, she found her mother mopping up something which had splattered up the red drapes. "I'm sure those curtains were a different colour," she remarked as she moved closer into the cold, log-fire encrusted room.

"Yes, they were, dear, I've had to had them changed several times now."

"Because of the dog?"

"No, I just couldn't decide on the colour. And besides, my predecessor had left them in a terribly crusty condition."

Sarah shuddered, thinking about Bates. Bastard. "And what happened now?"

"I spilt pasta down them."

"Pasta? You don't like pasta." She went to go sit down on the dark sofa on the right of the room. "Did you spill it down the side of the couch, as well?"

"Ah, yes."

"Mother, this isn't pasta, is it?"

"Ah, no."

"Then what is it?"

Mrs Jones moved from the curtains and sat at her desk. Not on her chair. Her desk. "Someone appears to have … used my study for … other … means." She pulled a face which both confused Sarah and made her perfectly aware of the situation.

"They've had sex in here?" Sarah stood up immediately. "Urgh - that's disgusting! I bet it was Dr Matthews and his boyfriend, if he could actually get one … he's so ugly he couldn't get one anyway."

"Actually, I think he's rather attractive. Got that sexy gay look about him."

"O*kay*. And what does Billy have to say about this?"

"Bobby?"

"Hmm."

"Oh, he's all in for threesomes. And it can't have been Russell. He has too many morals."

Sarah groaned. "Do you know who really did it in here?"

"No."

"Then I think I know."

"Who? It could help me, darling."

"I have no idea. But I could find out for you." Sarah inched herself down onto the soiled sofa again. "Hmm, yes, I think I could. What did you want to see me for, anyway?"

"Oh. Yes, that. Your sister."

"I don't have a sister. Bobby told me she died in France."

"Yes, that's true."

Sarah hit her hands against her head and subsequently moaned, purely because of it hurt and not due to her mother's infuriating, bull-headed bullness. She crossed and uncrossed her legs, as she found that the little dog was sniffing at her legs and she found it pleasurable for it to make whining noises when she wouldn't let it drool on her. Dog-hater she was not; she just disliked canines.

"What's he called?"

"It's a girl, isn't it? Oh, no, it's not. I got confused with the dangly bits." Sarah's mother chuckled a little. "I haven't got a name for him. I thought, because he keeps leaving his excretion all over the floor, I should call him David."

Sarah groped wildly for the relevance. She couldn't find it. She didn't question it. "Hmm. So … am I to get the bus home?"

"Yes, darling. I'm going to be a good couple of hours here. And didn't you have a date planned with that Andrew Cage chap?"

She squinted. "What?"

"You don't? Oh, it must be Maggie, then. I'll see you tonight, sunshine."

The phone was ringing when Sarah got home, and she was surprised that Tony hadn't bothered to get it. No, hold on. That didn't make any sense. She wasn't surprised in the slightest. If he'd known someone was going to call him, he wouldn't have answered the phone. He'd have let someone else answer it, being able to brag like hell that he was popular when he went to retrieve the phone-call. Ah, that make much more sense. Sarah breathed a silent sigh of relief.

It was Billy-Bob. "Hey, Sarah, honey, isn't your mother in?"

"Shouldn't that be … never mind. I'm sick of trying to lead a normal life. Let's all just be a little crazy, live a little. Have fun. Relax. Let the crazy stuff just *glide* over our heads."

"Sarah, dear … is your mother in?"

"No, she's still at work. Can I just ask you something?"

"Sure."

"Why do you always ring when you know my mother's at work?" She added, "I know you didn't know the first time, but after the first twenty phone-calls, you'd assume that you'd -"

"She's not in then?"

"No."

"I'll call back later."

She sensed he was going to hang up - she heard the swish of the phone and so she called out: "Wait!"

"Sarah?"

"Yes … um … I just wanted to know … uh … what is it that you do?"

"I'm a post man."

"A post man? Like, you deliver the post?"

"No," he replied truthfully, "I mend posts. You know, lamp posts and stuff."

"Really?" she asked, incredulous that anyone would actually have such a mundane job.

"No, Sarah, I was joking."

She felt like she'd walked into a room naked, and it wasn't a room in a naturist colony. Colony, my arse. "Oh, I see."

"And I'm a solicitor."

"What??"

"Post man by morning, solicitor by day. Good guy, then bad guy."

It was all too confusing for the girl. "Um, would you like to come for tea tomorrow? I'm sure we're not busy. You and Krystelle-May."

"That'd be lovely. It's supposed to be thundering. Shall I bring some steaks to put on the barbecue?"

Fifteen

It's All Looking Like A Cilla Black Studio In The Jones's House

"Where's the dog?"

"What, darling?"

Sarah's mother had been home an hour, and it was hitting half seven in the evening. They were sitting in the living room as a family; Sarah, Mrs Jones, Tony and Hannah. Sarah's father, Lesley, was somewhere insignificant.

The usual prime-time, much-publicised television soap opera - or long-lasting serial drama - was about to start, and Sam Jones was sitting on the sofa with her microwave meal on her lap.

"The dog. The little labrador."

"Ah, David? He's at the school."

There are often moments when it's difficult to understand what has just been said. It was a similar experience to being bollocked by a teacher or other lesser member of authority. Sarah was having one of those moments now. She screwed up her eyes. "You *what*?"

"David's in my study."

"Your - your *study*?! You left a little puppy in - in the study?" *Hold on,* she thought. *I am revealing hidden signs of puppy-itus? Am I a secret dog-lover?* Then she came to her senses: *Fuck it.*

"Yes, darling." Sam Jones tucked into her cauliflower cheese something-or-other. She had a little smile on her face. Sarah presumed it was because her mother had managed to switch on the microwave when it was already on anyway. Setting the time to cook the microwave meal was another story. Sarah had been the chef on that part.

"Oh, that's okay then."

It was Friday night, and Dr Matthews found himself sitting in a rank old pub in the town centre, moaning about the price of beer. It had risen considerably in the past few years, and his argument went: "All 'cos of that prime minister bitch."

“Sorry, mate, I don’t know you,” the guy sitting next to him said, “but I think you’re pretty much worse for wear.”

Russ looked to him left, catching a glimpse of his shiny silver watch - silver! The forty-seventh element of the Periodic Table! - and spotted that it was quarter to nine. Eight forty-five! How come, whenever he checked his watch, it was always a quarter to, or quarter past? And why did Americans - bless their rotting souls - use such bizarre time schemes? He looked back.

And why was that guy sitting next to him so damn sexy in his eyes?

“I have a problem,” Russ suddenly blurted out.

But the man sitting beside him had now vanished. Russ rubbed his head, his gelled hair, and then pondered where the rest of his group had buggered off to. He was quite, almost, most definitely positive that he had come out this evening with Iain Miller - who, by the way, was sticking to soft drinks following his two-heart-attacks-in-one-day marathon in July of this year. Dr Matthews had also been joined with his girlfriend or ‘fuck-chum’ (a phrase used so as not to get sued by major film corporations), Helen Moore. *Christ*, he thought as he rose to his feet unsteadily and possibly as steadily as he had ever been - after this many drinks (eleven), *she should’ve been named Jane. Plain Jain. Jane. Yeah, Jain. Like plain. Or Jane, like plane?* He realised how he could see the words spelt out in his mind was quite ingenious and he smiled as he tried to find the double doors to leave the pub.

Two minutes after Hannah and Tony crept up to his bedroom to ‘fool around’, as he put it (technically they were playing a board-game based on the streets in London), Sarah turned to her mother, who was now knitting a rice pudding.

"Oh, your boyfriend called earlier when you were out."

"Why didn't you put him on to me?" her mother asked, barely glancing up from the cream coloured wool which she had wound around her daughter's hands. The clacking of the two needles were the only things that separated Sam's words from the blare of the television.

"Because you were out."

"Oh." A gaping silence, and then: "What did he want?"

"I don't know, he wanted to talk to you. If he wanted to talk to me," the exasperated girl exclaimed, "then he would have told me what he wanted. But he didn't. He wanted to speak to you."

The snipping of the knitting needles began again. "Oh - and I invited him and his sister to dinner tomorrow night," Sarah added.

The wool and the knitting ensemble fell to the floor, leaving Sarah helplessly - and haplessly, it has to be said - holding the material tightly around vertically stretched hands. "You did what?"

"I thought it'd be a surprise for you."

Her mother was distraught. She stood, shaking, heart thumping … ah, no. That was her feet making the thudding on the patterned carpet. She slapped a hand to her head. "It is … oh … what … what can I feed them? But - but - oh, goats and monkeys!"

"Goats and …?"

"*Othello*, darling. You'll learn next year. You have impeccable timing, sweetheart. I already invited your Chemistry teacher over for dinner."

It was Sarah now who was standing shrieking now. "Dr Matthews? Dr Matthews? No! No!" She was hyperventilating. "But you can't! He's my teacher!

You can't invite a teacher to my house! My privacy! My place of solace, away from any reminders of S-H-C-O-O-L!" She screwed up her nose.

"But, darling - I work at the school too." Her mother re-seated herself.

Sarah folded her arms, then found it difficult to wipe away a piece of ebony hair. "Right. Something has to be done about that. You have to resign. Right now. Look," she said, flapping about like an emu, "I'll go get you a sheet of our headed paper. We can do a draft together. Write your resignation. Come on. For me."

Sarah fluttered her eyelashes.

"Stop fluttering your eyelashes."

She did. "Please!"

"Darling, I work there, and you'd best just get used to the idea."

Sarah sulked, folding her arms again. She inched her way back onto the sofa. "Who else have you invited?"

"Mr Miller."

"Aw!"

Sam Jones raised her brows. "And Mr Burch. Mrs Macintosh. But she can't come. Something about a hospital appointment to correct her voice." She cleared her throat. "And … that new I.T. technician."

"Mr Dover?"

"Yes, Ben."

Sarah shook her head, "He's not new."

"He's new to me. And I want you to be present, young lady. No sneaking off to meet your boyfriend." She caught her daughter's expression. "Oh, yes. I know all about this Andrew Cage fellow."

“Mother,” her daughter replied with a snort, rather sarcastically, “he doesn’t know I exist.”

“He didn’t say that in my office earlier today.”

Now Sarah was interested. “What?”

“He came into my study this morning. He had a letter from his parents about having a day off next Wednesday. The 26th October.”

“Thanks, I know the date next week.”

“Bet you couldn’t just think of it like that,” her mother answered, snapping her fingers a little too late. “I remember the date, because the two was written curly and … hold on, it could’ve been the twenty-fifth.”

“Whatever! What did he say about me?”

“You’d been giving him one-on-one Chemistry lessons because Mr Miller was teaching him. As if that had some significance - or as if I was supposed to understand. Anyway … I said we were having a little shin-dig on Saturday night. Wondered if he’d like to join us for a drinkie. Naturally, I’d turn a blind eye, what with him being under-age and all.”

Sarah couldn’t answer. “You asked out Andrew Cage for me? What did he say?”

“No.”

Her heart snapped in half, melted, and drizzled through the rest of her body. Sarah’s mother saw her discomfort. “I was joking, you daft half-penny.”

“I think the expression is - never mind.”

Sixteen

Hannah Achieves What Everyone Else Has Failed To Do

Meanwhile, up in Tony's bedroom, he picked up one of the dies - dices - a member of the dice amalgamation - whatever, and sucked on it thoughtfully. "Does it ever seem like your life has been paused, as if someone's studying it closely? Analysing it? By God, that's a big word."

Hannah groaned and raked a hand through her dark red hair. "If this is your theory that we're not real people and we're just concoctions of some weird writer's imagination, then you're wrong. Look," she slapped herself on the leg lightly, then poked her boyfriend. "We're both real. We're not fictional!"

"Then how come everything we say if perfect? How come we don't mistales - mistakes - when we talk? Like everything's been planned out?"

"Tony, I've started taking the Pill."

That shut the bastard up. She smiled widely.

"Bur-hur-wha?"

"I went to the doctors. He prescribed me the Pill. 'Cos I asked for it. And I think you're slightly frustrated because you keep coming out with shit - like you have verbal dysentery. And I bet you can't spell that, 'cos even I can't. Took me several seconds to even think of how to pronounce it." She smiled again. "Now, honey-bunch, shall we permanently pause this game of cheating to win fake money, or continue?"

"Um."

"Hmm. Just as I thought." Hannah carefully lifted the board onto Tony's desk, which he didn't use and was littered with crap. "And that doesn't mean that I'm going to just straight into bed with you. Even though we have been 'sleeping together' for the past three nights." She added, "Hasn't your mother asked yet why I keep appearing in the morning in my pyjamas?"

"No, she's always at work. Don't you notice that she's never there when you come down in the morning?"

"No."

"There we go, then."

Hannah beamed. "And my family haven't come searching for me. So everything's working out fine. Now. You were going to lie down and confess you have feelings for me."

Seventeen

Talullaah Becomes Confused … Could It Have Been The Vodka & Coke?

It was Friday night, obviously, because morning hadn't occurred yet. Talullaah Ali, who so far has seemed not predominant in this little catastrophe of a tale, was sitting in a pub in town, sipping at a vodka and coke which she was pretending was rum and coke, purely because vodka was so *out* this year.

Opposite her was seated a rather bladdered Dr Matthews. Talullaah had a talent of being able to drink several alcoholic beverages and be able to spot a loser. Being a strict Muslim, she shouldn't've been out at such a late hour (half ten), but she had things to do, people to meet, and a kilo's worth of smack to flog.

She had met up with him purely by coincidence, stalking him from the very moment he stepped out of his town apartment which was situated close to the

Grammar School, until this moment in some seedy little 'chic' public house. Now he was moaning about something or other.

"… and then he just vanished, like magic, in front of me. And I was like, woah, if you don't do blow-jobs you could've just told me. And the whole pub was like those pieces of hard plastic you play with as a kid. I kept walking into the walls, but I wasn't. The walls were walking into *me.*"

Talullaah sighed. "Listen, Dr Matthews, I have some more of those magazines on me if you want to see them." They were seated in the middle of the pub, where they were hidden from all's sight. "Do you want to see them?"

He nodded like a … what were they called again? Chimpan- well, he couldn't quite remember, and besides, he wasn't the one looking at himself. He scratched his gelled, dark brown hair. "Is my hair going?"

"No, Dr Matthews."

"Oh."

She reached into her large, new black and pink, *Billy Bag* ... er … bag, and brought out the latest copy of *Big and Beefy*. "Here. Eighteen quid."

"But -"

"Eighteen pounds sterling, Dr Matthews. None of that Euro crap. Like anyone uses that bollocks."

"No one does 'cos it's not legal tender!"

He was too drunk to care, and accepted the fact that she simply pocketed the twenty without giving him the change for another drink.

When the bell rang, Talullaah was being bored out her mind by Dr Matthews talking shite about Sarah Jones and his preoccupation about her being called 'Maggie'. He was lying back on the sofa-chair thing, ranting. Suddenly, without the slightest hint of warning, the conversation changed direction.

Talullaah slammed herself upright on the chair, tucking into her scarf escaped pieces of dark hair. "What did you just say?"

"I said," he exhaled with effervescence, a word which no doubt he wouldn't be able to read in the state he was in, never mind pronounce, "that Sarah's got a secret that she doesn't know anything about."

"How can she have a secret if she doesn't know what it is?" the young Muslim girl asked, legs crossed, leaning in towards the teacher. "I thought that was the whole reason of having a secret. To keep it to yourself. Unless, of course, you're someone like your sister, who blabs any slither of crap she hears to all and sundry."

"Who's Sundry?"

"A relative of mine who's in the year below," she ad-libbed. "Anyway, about this secret."

"Oh, yeah."

"Well?" she persisted. She was leaning in quite close to the teacher now, and thankfully her chest and cleavage was covered up by the highly infectious designer top she was wearing.

He twiddled at his undone top button. "She has a secret twin sister."

She gasped. "It's true, then?"

"What do you know?" he asked, moving closer to her like he was about to pass her another twenty pounds so she could give him a further gay porn magazine, which, naturally, he was doing.

She clutched the two tenners, put them in her purse and then handed over another slick glossy … she was sure that it would become a lot more slick and glossy once he'd took it back to his apartment later.

"I know she has a twin sister."

"How?"

"Because you just told me."

"Ah." He looked confused, then mildly settled. "I see. Is that all you know?"

She itched her eyebrow. "I don't know."

"What d'you mean, you don't know? Either you know more or you don't. Like I know that Sarah's sister's called Maggie, she's been living in France for most of her life, and that she's being slowly worked back into Sarah's life even though Maggie's not allowed at the school. What do you know?"

"Er … Sarah's sister's called Maggie, she's been living in France for most of her life, and that she's being slowly worked back into Sarah's life even though Maggie's not allowed at the school," she echoed. Copy and paste, simply copy and paste.

"How do you know that?"

She smiled, "You just told me, Dr Matthews."

"And anyway, I'm thinking of writing a dyslexic joke book," Tony was saying as he and his girlfriend continued not to play the board game which conveniently still on his table of doom.

"What?"

"A joke book. About dyslexic people."

Hannah raised her brows. "You do it, if you think that'll be a good idea. Have you got any sample material?"

He nodded enthusiastically. "Yeah, lots. Okay. First joke -"

"Wait: don't tell me it's that very un-original one about the dyslexic, agnostic, insomniac?"

He shook his head. "No. A man walked into a bar. 'Ouch!'"

It took several seconds to allow the horrible, pathetic number of words of the joke sink into her mind. "What? That's horrendous! That's got nothing to do with dyslexia!"

"Oh, but it has. You just have to think about it a lot."

Hannah sat there on the bed, thinking. She wracked her brain for any thoughts that emerged about the 'joke'. "I give up."

"Well, um … well … it's quite difficult to explain. Um …"

"You don't know, do you?"

"Nope."

Hannah sighed and lay back on the bed.

"So, to summarise: Sarah Jones has a twin sister who has been living in France for most of her life, and now, for some bizarre reason, she has had enough of old frog-country, and wants to enter our sham of a country." Talullaah was counting nothing on her fingers; she just thought she looked good with her long, smooth digits. "Sarah knows nothing. So what happens next?"

Dr Matthews looked a little glazed-over, and for a swift moment, Talullaah half-hoped that he was dead so that she wouldn't have to drag him out of the pub half-conscious. Then again, if he was dead -

That was as far as her thoughts went. Dr Matthews stirred and rubbed his face. "Urghghshuhgifgh," he said. Which isn't a real word and requires a squiggly red line. As does squiggly.

"What?"

"I said, yes, that's true, Miss Ali."

She tapped her long nails on the dirty pub table. "Hmm. I asked a question and you reply in a non-sense making manner. Makes complete sense. What happens next? When does Sarah get to find out about her sister?"

"She doesn't."

He studied her expression. She looked as pissed off as he felt pissed. And needed to piss. He smiled at her. "Mrs Jones is trying to keep it as best a secret as she can. Even though Maggie keeps popping up at school."

"Grrrr."

"Talullaah?"

"I've been sitting here with you what seems like hours -"

"It has been."

"Whatever. And I haven't learnt a thing apart from everything else you've told me." She touched her material-covered head and scratched her hair hopefully. "You're drunk and I can't even get anything out of you."

He smiled again. "I'm good, aren't I?"

"No, hopeless. Well … if you're not going to reveal anything else to me, then I'd best be off. School on Monday?" she asked by way of a good-bye. Typically, it was misinterpreted. Arse.

"It usually is. Apart from Bank Holidays. But most of them are in the school holidays any -"

She heard no more, as she had already sped away from the teacher and out of the rapidly emptying pub.

It seemed like Friday would never end.

Surprisingly, it did.

Eighteen

Vomituous

Saturday morning arrived, and there was nothing anyone could do about it. Not even Sarah, who awoke moaning at seven with one stinking hell of a hangover, purely achieved by drinking several pints of lemonade. Sugar-induced. Apart from the fact that she was awake, she felt comatose.

Rolling out of bed on that mid-October morning, she tried to recollect, like a post-drunk Chemistry teacher, just what exactly she had been up to the previous night. Ah, yes. Sitting in the living room most of the night with her mother, the HEADMISTRESS, whilst hearing the dreadful words that came out of her mouth: shit, she couldn't remember. Damn her sieve-like memory. Nevertheless, she knew that there was something strange about how it was still dark this morning, and suddenly Sarah was swept up in the fact that it was Autumn. Hallowe'en was on its way, (yippee! Egg-chucking time!), then her favourite of all times of the year, Bonfire Night (naturally). Next came Christmas, which she didn't fully understand.

Autumn. Only a while ago it was Summer. Next was Winter. She smiled at her intelligence. Frowning, she heard a tremendous knocking at her door. When she moved across her bedroom carpet towards the exit - and entrance - she opened it to find the slight bulk of Hannah Simpson, their current tenant.

"Oh my God, Sarah. You look really ill!"

"Hangover."

"But me and Tony drank the last of the lager."

"Lemonade."

"Ahh. Um … what are you doing today?"

Hannah was dressed in Tony's only shirt, a remnant from his school-days after the rest were burnt in a ritual bonfire with all of his school-books. She looked frail, afraid, and pretty. Sarah inwardly growled.

"Huh?" She wiped under her panda-eyes, then thought. "No, not doing anything. Why?"

"Do you want to go shopping? I nicked one of my father's credit cards when I ran away, so I've got five grand to throw away."

"Why don't you just cut the card up and flush it down the toilet?" she asked, still weary.

"No, I mean, we can go spend his money. All five grand of it."

"Five thousand pounds?" Sarah asked, "How much does your dad make a month?"

"Less than your dad."

"My who?" Sarah sighed. "Oh, Lesley. I haven't seen him in days. Wonder where he is. Oh well. Sure. I'll go shopping with you. But … I've got, like, a strange feeling that something's not right. Something bad's going to happen." She felt bile rush up her throat, and she sped to the bathroom, where she was promptly sick. Vomituous, if you will. A word to put in the dictionary, because apparently it isn't there at the moment.

"I'll have another coupla' hours sleep, okay?" called Hannah from Sarah's bedroom door.

Russ Matthews opened his eyes at around nine and then decided it would be best if he closed them again. The light from his open curtains which he couldn't recall opening last night was piercing, ramming itself into his eyeballs and even eyelids like some kind of hostile, gaseous alien life-form. He rolled over and heard his sister Lucy patter outside his bedroom.

What was she doing up at this time? It was Saturday morning, not a school day. Or was she going to - ? And what was that singing? He wondered whether he should go investigate. Nah, leave her to it. But singing? That tune from a Disney cartoon?

Russ creaked open the bedroom door, still dressed in the clothes he had been wearing the previous night. And what exactly had happened last night? He checked his anal muscles - nope, perfectly in order and no pain at all. He unclenched the muscles and spotted his chubby bottle-blonde sister scrambling eggs.

She spotted him second, but spoke first. "Good morning, Russ. How are you this morning?"

Hmm. All the curtains and blinds were drawn, the former even tied back with the things that tied them back. Something was definitely going on. "Lucy?"

"Yes? Scrambled eggs for breakfast?"

"Have we got any headache tablets?"

"What for?"

"My headache."

She 'hmmed' to herself. "I don't know. What did you get up to last night? Had a few drinks with your fellow colleagues?"

"Yeah, something like that."

She was now placing the bowl in the microwave, humming to herself softly. He truly did feel ill, and it wasn't solely due to his de-hydrated brain … or whatever. Science had never been his thing on a Saturday morning.

"I opened your curtains this morning. You didn't notice."

He nodded, and moved towards the kitchen table which was placed in the middle of the room. There was a jug of fresh orange juice in the centre of the table, with tall transparent glass stood rigidly next to it. He went to sit down, but paused, mid-sit, due to the object which he found propped up against the vase of dried flowers he'd allocated a spot for a week ago.

The magazines.

"Gur-hudfh-adkhr-sdfih," he got out. No translations please.

"What's the matter, big bro?" Lucy asked sweetly, pressing buttons on the microwave.

Maybe she hadn't noticed. Maybe last night, he'd come in and placed them there, lying in wait for this morning, not believing that Lucy would be up at this time. But it was a risk. And there was that awful stench of victory and humiliation in the air - or was that toast and over-frazzled egg?

Lucy listened to the beeps of the microwave, and then in a daze, Russ watched her slam the scrambled eggs on two slices of buttered, white toast. His vision had become misty, almost as if tears had formed in his eyes and were now dripping slowly down his cheeks. He looked to the unvarnished, beech coloured table - or beach coloured table - and saw spots of darkness.

Lucy placed the food in front of him, masking the tears for the time being. "There you go. And I've already made photocopies of them, so don't think you've got away with anything."

For a moment there, Russ was convinced his sister was talking about the scrambled eggs. But his mind switched back into semi-normal mode and he inhaled the sickly stench of the eggs and realised that he could be faced with the biggest humiliation of his life.

He raced to the toilet, where he, too, was greatly vomituous.

Nineteen

Talullaah Calls

Vomit was an interesting thing, when you thought about it. Mind you, when Sarah thought about it on Saturday morning, she found herself being rushed by her medium-built legs to the nearest public toilet, the vomit expressing itself in the most disgusting means possible. As if advertising itself, the sick would rise up in her throat, making her gip, before finally emerging, victorious, into the nearest hole. A perfect sale.

Hannah was dumb-struck at how much stuff her boyfriend's sister had in her stomach. They were in the town together, trying to shop for clothes - naturally - and trying was the best used word. Every time they stepped into one of the warm, non air-conditioned shops, the raven-haired girl spun round and chased her own feet to a fast-food outlet where she could use the public toilets without having to buy anything, the workers not caring less. It was a simple trick, but one that back-fired on her; most of the toilets were up a flight of stairs and Sarah often had the rancid liquid mixture - compound? It was chemically bonded, she supposed - spurting out of her mouth.

Hannah was busy continuously thinking about vomit - the vomit which was continuously flowing from her boyfriend's sister's large yet dainty mouth. Sarah herself was no longer thinking of the sick, her mind was on other things such as how *not* to be vomituous.

"Are you pregnant?" Hannah finally asked once they had sat down for a second outside a major designer label shop. "Because you're acting like it. Puking up all morning, having sex with every other person and teacher - no, hold on, that's

Marie, isn't it? And being awfully moody whenever anyone mentions Andrew Cage and your little 'date' tonight."

"What? No one ever mentions Andrew Cage, and *what* little date tonight? Sorry, 'date'?" Sarah looked over at Hannah from the rusty old new bench they were sitting on. "And since when have you become the hard-arse? You've always been such a quiet, strange girl, with scars all over her arms and not talking to anyone. And since you've starting going out with my brother, you've turned normal. And I don't like that. It's not right for you to be normal. You're Hannah Simpson."

"Sarah Jones," she said, as means of a sarcastic introduction.

"No, *I'm* Sarah Jones."

"Stop being a stroppy cow. I do have a personality, you know. People just couldn't be arsed finding it out because everyone just *loves* normality, *loves* it when people act all the same like fucking cows -"

"Sheep."

"Shut up correcting me," Hannah snapped. "I'm sick and tired of your 'oh, my life is so unreal' routine. 'Ohh, the headmaster tried to rape me', 'ohh, Andrew Cage will never fancy me when I'm just standing here doing nothing', 'ohhh, I have a twin sister that no one told me about but everyone knows about.'"

"What? How do you know that?"

"I have been living in your house for quite a few days now. I do pick up on the conversations. I'm such an Iago."

"A what? What's an e-yago?"

"Never mind." Hannah touched her burning forehead lightly. Hang on, wasn't it Sarah who was ill? Had she suddenly spread her illness in a matter of hours to her, or had Sarah got her more mad than she'd like to admit?

"Oh, you're pissing me off now," Hannah muttered, and reached for her mobile phone. It began to ring just as she pulled it out of her little bag. *Talullaah*. Thank God for that.

"Hello?"

"Hey, Hannah, it's me."

"Hi, me. What's up?"

Talullaah smirked, although surprisingly Hannah couldn't see it. "I've got some shockingly funny news. Are you on your own?"

"I might as well be," she muttered, tapping her fingers on the bench, irritated. She took a glance at Sarah, who was turning a paler shade of white. "What was the news?"

Talullaah giggled, probably sitting in her bedroom with her hair out, flicking through a copy of *Hard and Horny* just for the fun of it before she flogged them tonight. "Well, Sarah Jones …"

"Um … yeah?"

"Guess who I bumped into last night in the pub?"

"Um …" Hannah hesitated, looking over at her boyfriend's sister again. "The girl whom you just mentioned?"

"No, silly. None other than Dr Matthews."

"You keep 'bumping' into him quite a lot."

Talullaah giggled again. "Yeah, he buys all the male-porn off me. Anyway, he got drunk on two glasses of coke again … nah, I'm only joking, more like three half-pints of lager … and told me that Sarah *does* have a twin sister. You know there was all those rumours that she did?"

"Uh-huh?" she asked, feeling a burning on her neck like someone was talking about her. Strange.

"Yeah, well, 'tis true. As true as the Koran. That's the Muslim holy book, by the way," she informed Hannah.

"I know, I had to do it for a spare GCSE lesson."

"Oh, well, I just learnt last week at the place we go to worship."

"Mosque?" Hannah asked, touching her hair a little to straighten it.

"Hey, you're good! Anyway … you'd better ask Tony more about this, what with her being his sister and all. But she's come back to England from France, where she's been living most of her life. Looks the spitting reflection of Sarah. Wants to come back to school! Imagine that!" She laughed again. "Now wouldn't that just royally piss Dr Matthews off! Two identical Sarahs to get on his tits!"

Hannah laughed back. "Yeah, yeah. Well, I'll ask him this afternoon. See what he says. I'd better go, anyway. I'll see you on Monday."

"See you later."

When they simultaneously hung up, Sarah smiled meekly at Hannah. "Who was that?"

"No one you know. Any, um, way … weren't you feeling ill? Should we go home now?"

"We've only been here a few minutes."

"An hour, Sarah."

"Yeah, sixteen minutes."

"Sixty."

"No, sixteen, Hannah. They changed it, don't you remember?"

Hannah pulled a face and dragged a weak Sarah to her feet. "I don't know what planet you're from. Come on. I have to speak with your brother."

Twenty

Finally, It All Becomes Unclear!

Hannah threw her bag and body onto her boyfriend's bed after the non-successful trip into town. Sarah had sloped into her bedroom, moaning of feeling sick - which she had threatened to show her mother by giving her a novel demonstration - whilst leaving Hannah to join Tony in his bedroom.

"Tony," began the red-head as she breathed evenly, "can I ask you a question?"

"It depends," her boyfriend remarked, coming out of the closet where he had been fishing around for clothes for this evening; a difficult task. "What type of a question is it? If it's anything to do with English, you're buggered."

"What? Why?"

"Well, I'm dyslexic, aren't I?"

Hannah shrugged. "I'm not so sure. Anyway, it's nothing to do with English. Apart from the fact you speak the language." She took in a deep breath, unsure where to continue. She wanted to discuss the fact that his sister had a twin. She wanted it to come out quickly, frankly, honestly, naturally, but no matter how many words in the dictionary and/or thesaurus there are, it wasn't going to happen. And didn't the old saying go: I want never gets? Bollocks to that.

"It's a rather … uh-hum … personal question."

Tony scratched his head, a motion that Hannah had grown to used to and now adored. Apart from the fact that her boyfriend was wearing only boxer shorts and it was getting on for lunch-time.

"Seven inches," he replied. "About eighteen centimetres, if you want to be metre-ric."

Hannah screwed her eyes up. "You're putting that on. You're putting on you're dyslexic, aren't you?"

"No -"

"That's not dyslexia, Tony."

“But -”

“You’re just lazy.”

“But -”

He sighed. “Well, I want to ask you a personal question. When are we going to have sex, eh?”

She just looked at him. If anyone else female has been asked that question, they know the precise look - glare - she offered him. “How’s your dyslexic joke book coming on?”

“Is that *it*?”

“No, but … just answer the question.”

Tony pulled on a T-shirt that he found on the floor (an easy cotton and lycra treasure chest). “Fine. Now what was the one I thought of … I wrote them down. But then when I came to reading them, I couldn’t read what it said. Dammit.” He moved to his desk of crap and haplessly tried searching for the crap. Looked easy. However, he had no luck.

“*Any*way …” She went on, “Hold on a sex. Sec.” Hannah moved to shut the door, and she could practically feel him jump on her. However, Tony leaped onto the bed, obviously thinking that he was going to get a good whuppin’. Sorry, Mr King. She groaned. “I’m not having sex with you whilst your mother is downstairs preparing the food for tonight. Not like that has anything to do with anything. I need to talk with you privately. About Sarah.”

“Am I going to have to put some clothes on for this?”

She raised her brows. “Just sit up , for God’s sake.”

He did so. “What’s the matter?”

Pinching her lips together, Hannah managed to speak. Of course, after her lips were re-opened. "Talullaah rang me today. Ironically, this morning, when I was with Sarah in town."

"And?"

Strangely enough, Tony was now beginning to believe that something was wrong and upsetting Hannah. It didn't even take her the three signs: slapping him, pouring water over him, or crying.

"And she told me that Sarah has a twin sister."

"And?"

"And that she's lived in France most of her life, which Sarah hasn't known about. Or you. And now she's back in England, wanting to go to school here. Yes, I know. Horrible."

"And?"

"Oh, stop saying that. It's not funny. You look like a goldfish. Saying 'and' all the time makes you look like a constipated goldfish."

Tony looked at his lap. He didn't answer.

"Sorry … I didn't mean to … offend you," she went on. "But I thought you'd've been called worst things than that before." What was it? Sensitive about fish? Something to do with Marie? Her fishiness? Disgusting. What a thought. Or internal monologue. Had he had a goldfish once, that he'd lost? Goldie? Had he been cleaning him out and accidentally flushed him down the toilet?

"Tony?"

He shook his head. She reached for his chin, yanking up his head. He cried out in pain and rubbed at his neck. "You don't have to be so vivacious."

"Vicious."

"Bitch." He exhaled. "The thing is … I already knew all that that you told me."

"What?"

He scratched his head. "I knew she has a twin sister. I don't know why you don't know, anyway. It might as well be all across the school. Dr Matthews knows."

"I know." She winced at the repetition and promised to read a few pages of the thesaurus tonight. "But … why does he know?"

Tony bit his lip and scratched his head again.

"Stop it, you'll bleed!"

He stopped, for the sake of his wrist, which Hannah was clutching at with middle-length nails digging into his skin. "Okay, okay. But you won't believe me."

"I will, I will."

"He's their father."

Hannah began to laugh. "Piss off! You lie!"

"I knew you wouldn't believe me," he said, sulking.

"But Dr Matthews is gay!"

"Camp. And that doesn't mean anything, anyway."

Hannah stifled a giggle. "Besides, how old would that make him when he shagged your mother? Ten?"

Tony rolled his eyes. "Seventeen. Perfectly legal."

"And your mum was how old?"

"Twenty-two. Five years older than him."

Hannah was confused. "But … he doesn't act like he's her father."

"He doesn't know."

"What??"

Tony stretched his legs out. "Surprise, surprise, he was drunk when it happened." He laughed at that. "Absolutely plastered. Couldn't remember a thing. I don't even know where it happened."

"Tony," she said slowly, "you're not just lying, are you, to make up a good plot-line?"

"Why would I want to do that?"

She shrugged. "So … it still doesn't make sense. Why send just one daughter away?"

"She was twenty-two. Twenty-three, nearly. She hardly had a career going for her. She could barely cope with one child. Maggie just drew the short stick."

"Straw."

"Yeah, that."

"What about your dad?" she asked. "Don't tell me …"

"No, no. I don't even know who my parents are."

"What??"

"I'm adopted."

Sarah lay on her bed, inched the covers on her, and slept until half past seven.

She woke at the above-mentioned hour, solely because she felt her brother's warm hands shaking her. "Sarah, Sarah. Wake up. The guests are going to be here soon."

"What guests?" As a matter of fact, why wake up? And what guests? Ah, yes, she'd already said that.

"Dr Matthews, Mr Burch, Mr Miller, Ben Dover … come on, I know how much you fancy him."

"And your mother's boyfriend and Krystelle-May's coming too. And Andrew Cage." Those words of evil came from Hannah, looking pretty in pink. Or - no, that was black.

"Andrew Cage?" Sarah sat herself up. She felt sicker than before. She pushed past the two of them and threw up in the bathroom toilet.

They told her not to bother coming down, but she pressed on, wanting to see Andrew and tell him she fancied him like fuck and wanted to have his babies. She stepped into the kitchen, her sight blurred a little, and had to hold on to the door-frame.

Sarah spotted a dark head in the dining room with someone she suspected was her mother. When she moved into the dining room, feeling like the younger Michael Myers in *Halloween*, wearing a mask, she noticed that it was *only* her mother in the room. She was feeling extraordinarily dizzy. If only she could reach for the chair …

"Sarah? Are you all right?"

"Where is everyone?"

With a distraction by her aching stomach, she managed to glance down at herself, making her head spin even more, and saw that she was still wearing the vomituous clothes from this morning. Of course, she'd slept a good few hours and hadn't had chance to get changed.

"Everyone's in the lounge, sweetie."

Lounge, is it now? "Oh. What about Andrew Cage?"

"He's in there too. Looking around for you. Worried you weren't going to come down."

She nodded. "I'll go … go … see him. Better show my face. Especially to the teachers, ho ho." Slowly, she made her way into the living room.

"And we did it right in the study! Over the desk, and then the bloody sofa! We didn't have any tissues or anything to clean the cack up … let's face it, it was most of hers …" Ben Dover the I.T. technician was commenting. "Catholic my arse. She's a horny little bitch."

What? What was he saying? And in front of Andrew, a pupil? She searched the brightly lit room, the lights hitting her eyes like baseballs of neon swung by a master batsman, and couldn't find him. "Andrew?" she croaked out.

"Oh, he's in the bog," Mr Burch was saying. He had a Yorkshire accent today. Lovely. "He'll be out in a tick, don't you worry, love."

She didn't have the strength to raise her eyebrows. "Oh." She stepped out of the living room, realising that Dr Matthews and Mr Miller hadn't even acknowledged her. Oh well, it was for the best.

In her blurry madness, as if she hadn't had anything to eat in days, or hadn't slept in weeks, she saw a flash of chocolate brown - two flashes, in fact - and guessed that Bobby and his sister (the bitch, she recalled), must have passed by her. She felt like a ghost. Yet why couldn't she walk through walls?

Sarah had the bizarre feeling that something terrible wasn't going to happen. Let's face it, what could be worse than thinking you were dying? Knowing you were dying, no doubt. Urgh. What a bloody thought.

A hammer against her head shook her awake.

"Oh, who could that be?" she heard her mother call out a few dozen corridors away. "Sarah, darling, could you get that?"

"Shhure," she slurred. In fact, what she said was, "Sure." So, no slurring at all. What an interesting language. Sarah shifted to the front door, her feet aching, her mind paining her more. Worst of all was her gut. She had to repeatedly keep checking her stomach hadn't been slit and that her intestines were still in place.

She saw nothing through the glass of the front door. Not because her eyes were shut, which they were, but because it was pitch black. Oh, and because her eyes were shut. She opened them, switched on the outside light, and saw a girl outside. Hmm, a bit scratty. Wearing snobby clothes. Sarah pressed her forehead against the glass, simply as the material was so beautifully cool. About five foot five. Slim. Middle-length, jet black hair. What an old hair-style! God, almighty.

And who was it? She cupped her hands around her face to get a better look. She didn't seem that familiar. Sarah wished she could just lean against the glass all night, but it was getting warm, and no doubt in the October coldness, the girl outside was gradually freezing her nuts off.

Sarah unlocked the door and opened it, stumbling a little.

"Hi. You must be Sarah. Finally. We meet. I'm your twin sister. Maggie."

Sarah opened her eyes wider. "Are - you - wearing - my Calvin Klein skirt?" She couldn't take in another breath. She fainted.

Hearing the commotion in the kitchen, Mrs Jones came to see what the fuss was about. She saw her daughter on the floor and tried to step over her. A hand appeared on her shoulder. Richard Burch.

Richard spotted the unconscious girl, looked across at the headmistress again, and said, "So when's dinner ready? I'm starved."

Twenty-one

Yossarian

And there was suddenly an amalgamation of voices which Sarah couldn't differentiate between. Words such as 'amalgamation' and 'differentiate' were popping into her head. It was black. She felt coldness pressing up against the back of her head, like lying in a pool of recently defrosted urine.

"Why isn't she coming round?"

"How long should I heat this up in the microwave for?"

"Slap her a bit."

"How come you're not a doctor if you've got a psychology degree?"

“Why don’t you act more like you’re dyslexic if you’re supposed to be?”

“Just slap her.”

“I’m not slapping her.”

Her mother’s voice. Good. Her mother wasn’t going to be using any force on her. Thank God.

“But this egg beater should do the trick.” Her mother’s voice again.

A camp voice, saying: “I’ve phoned the ambulance. You know, Sam, it really is a hazard having wooden paneling on your kitchen floor. Blood can completely ruin it.”

“Mind you, this one doesn’t seem to be much of a bleeder.” Her mother.

Silence again. Sarah ached to open her eyes, but the pain was too much. And she seemed to believe that if she opened her eyes, she’d want to be unconscious again. But hold on - wasn’t she unconscious now?

Words wouldn’t pass her lips. All she could get out was a moan. Then she began to dream again.

In her dream, her mother and Dr Matthews were having rampant sex in the back of a car whilst she watched, almost from the height of a baby sitting in a carry-seat. Blushing, she managed to wince herself away from the ungodly scene, cheeks flushing velvet purple (don’t ask me where *that* came from), and into her brother’s bedroom.

“Tony … what’s going on? Why’s my fucking Chemistry teacher fucking fucking our fucking mother?” She put her hand to her mouth to stop the obscenities from leaking out. Leaking - more like gushing from a sink that had been attacked with a sledgehammer.

He didn't speak a word. Her brother, however, to her ultimate disgust and vomituous-ness, pressed her up against his recently painted wall and began kissing her. She felt his hard … urgh … *thing* … press into her. Urgh, urgh - God! Of all the brother's she didn't have, she'd never been attracted to Tony … he was so much like her for a start, and …

So why was she kissing him back?

"It's … incest …" she managed to choke out through his … hmmm … stimulating kisses. Christ, is this what Hannah had to put up with? And Marie? Where was Marie? She hadn't seen her for a while. She was probably off shagging that I.T. technician …

"How can it be incest? We're not related!"

"Even if that's true," Sarah remarked, "you're the last person I'd ever want to … do … urgh … *anything* with. Christ … my mind is bloody messed up to be dreaming this!"

Tony ignored what she said and came out with: "You're not my sister, and dad's not your dad. Happy now?"

She noticed his mouth was smudged after he had kissed her hard, red from pressing up against her. "They must have put me on drugs. No one dreams like this unless they're on medication. Nobody."

"You are on medication, Sarah, you were knocked unconscious when you fainted."

"Huh? That makes no sense whatsoever. And I've getting out of here. Concussion or no concussion, I rarely dream but I've pretty sure I can control this one."

She wandered out of her brother's room and into her own, still feeling like she wanted to be sick and washed the taste of his mouth out with hydrochloric acid. Yum. Andrew Cage was lying on her bed, naked.

"You know, if all this shit that's happened in this dream turns out to be true, then I'm a very lucky person," Sarah said to herself. She moved closer to Andrew, who, she noticed faintly (his penis was more interesting, as a matter of fact) that he'd had his hair cut shorter. *For me.*

"No, 'cos it was getting in my eyes. I can read your thoughts, Sarah. This is a dream."

Sarah got onto the bed, thinking, *What the hell*, and sat on top of her pre-boyfriend. Oh, if only she could rip off all her clothes and take him right there. A sudden draft passed across her and she noticed that she - ha - was naked. Naked, in front of Andrew Cage. She blushed like she had earlier in her dream, and fell off him, breasts and all, and tried hopelessly to find an item of clothing to put on. All she could find was a Polaroid photograph of someone who looked liked Dr Matthews in his younger years. *Dad* was scrawled on the white area in marker pen.

She glanced back at Andrew. He had crossed his legs, arms folded, and was sitting up, watching her. "What do you know about this? What do you know?"

"More than anyone else? Not a thing."

That's not a good thing.

"Nope, Sarah, it isn't."

She zoomed backwards out of the room, just after noticing a particular area of Andrew's skin where she'd like to lick - just under his collar bone, where a chicken-pox scar (or small pox, who knew?) grazed his skin.

She felt his kiss on her mouth even as she was moving down the stairs backwards, falling, falling, tripping over air, until she hit the bottom and -

"Where the fucking hell am I? Where the bastard hell is my mother? And why the fucking fucked up twatting hell have I got tubes coming out of places I didn't know existed?"

"She's like the kid out of *The Exorcist*," came a hushed voice.

Sarah was sitting up, sweating, after waking from a nightmare, almost in the identical way that nobody in real life woke up like, yet so flawlessly managed to do so in films and bad fiction.

Her vision seemed glassy - not gassy - like a badly blurred photograph and yet she could still make out the bizarre shapes of some of the people in the hospital - hospital! - room with her. Her mother.

What was she doing here?

"Sarah Jones, I do *not* wish to hear you use language like that again!" Huffing, her mother's face was a mauve colour. Or perhaps that was the drugs. That her Mrs Jones was on, naturally.

A hand touched Sam Jones's bony shoulder. "Eh, Sam, don't be too hard on her. She's had a rough time, falling over and such like."

Sarah shook her head slightly. Who was talking with such a moronic accent? She narrowed her eyes and focused. Dr Matthews. Dr *Matthews*? Since when did he visit pupils in hospital?

Then it all came spinning back to her. As she closely detected the people in front of her: her mum, Dr Matthews, her brother (which made her blush, she couldn't recall why), and Andrew Cage, all looking worried and tired, she realised what had happened.

“Where’s my f - my skirt? Where’s my skirt?” she asked.

Bobby appeared out of nowhere. Her mother’s lover exhaled and folded his arms. “If you’re talking about your sister, then she’s outside. Still wearing your skirt, I might add.”

Sarah gritted her teeth. “Bitch. But I don’t have a sister.”

Bobby walked out of the room, his two second appearance almost comical, leaving the only girl in the room with a stinking headache alone with some strange, strange folk. She touched her head. “I banged this bit, didn’t I?”

Dr Matthews nodded and seated himself on a plastic contraption - apparently a chair. “Yes, you collapsed. We’d like to think that, in all honest clichés, you fell over, fainting, because you saw your twin sister for the first time. But as this is real life …”

“It isn’t,” Sarah remarked.

“Whatever. Fiction, non-fiction, a work of art. What the doctor seems to think is that you had a slight case of a new illness, seemingly made up on the spot. It includes vomiting, dizziness, and loss of consciousness. Not pregnancy.”

“What have I got?”

“You don’t have anything,” Dr Matthews replied.

“Huh? Then why am I in hospital?”

“When you collapsed,” her mother cut in, “you banged your head on the wooden floor - tsk! - and you’ve had a touch of concussion.”

“But what the bollocks is Dr Matthews talking about then?”

There was a lengthy silence. All eyes were on the teacher. He finally spoke, eyes twitching a little as he nervously reached for his tie. Puff. "Um … the doctor told me … that you had a virus."

They all groaned. "Virus?" Sarah asked. "That's all they ever say." She decided to face no facts: "So … what's this about a sister?"

Twenty-two

It Was An Eventuality …

"You know what I've realised?" asked Hannah Simpson to Talullaah Ali the following morning as they sat in the waiting area outside Sarah's ward.

"What's that?" the Muslim girl replied, idly spotting Barbara wandering around with a bag of drugs in her hand; Barbara, the morphine addicted receptionist.

"Huh?"

"What have you realised?"

"That no-one's died recently. Don't you think it's time that someone died?"

Talullaah opened her eyes wide. "What? That's a horrible thing to say."

"But don't you think that … well … what if it's Sarah's turn?"

"To *die*?"

Hannah shrugged.

But Sarah wasn't dying. On the Sunday afternoon, she had been visited by several members of staff - hell knows why, she hated them all apart from Mrs Green (whom she feared, and, incidentally, *didn't* come to visit her), and was positively glowing.

Her mother decided to 'drop by' and see her only daughter - only meaning … er, one of two … and chat a little about Sarah's new sister.

"But why hasn't Dad said anything to me about it after almost seventeen years?" She added, puzzled, "Where is he, by the way? I haven't seen him in days."

"No idea. And he doesn't even know about Maggie. It's not his child."

Sarah knocked her head back. Her neck came with it. "What?"

"Maggie's father isn't … your father."

Sarah itched the back of her neck, irritated with her skin and mother. "I don't understand. If she's my twin sister - which I'm betting my life on -" If only Talullaah and Hannah could hear her say that! "- then how can Dad not be her dad?"

Sam shrugged, then looked away, her body squeaking on the formerly shiny plastic chair.

"Mother?"

Sam didn't answer.

"The only way that Dad isn't Maggie's dad, is if -"

"Yes, I know. Is if Tony isn't your brother."

Sarah moaned. "You're giving me headache. How on earth - what relevance does this have to … ohmigod … my dream."

"What?"

“Nothing. So … please, explain.” Inexplicable tears were beginning to form in Sarah’s eyes. “Why isn’t Maggie’s father my father? And why isn’t Tony my brother?”

Her mother swallowed. “Um … because your father isn’t your father. I just married him on a drunken whim one night during the swinging 80’s. His mate had a vicar-thing. Stupid thing.” A sigh. From both of them. “Look, darling, I could go all into the details of who your father is, and so forth, but it really wouldn’t matter. Or mean a thing to him.”

“Why?”

“Because he doesn’t know himself.”

Sarah raised her brows. “I don’t understand,” she answered wearily. “Why doesn’t he know?”

“He was … rather young at the time.”

“Well … who’s my bloody father, then?”

Her mother bit her lip, then replied: “Bobby.”

Twenty-three

Fatherless

"Bobby? How the hell is *Bobby* my *father*? Forgive me if I'm wrong, but Bobby is *black*."

Sam Jones scratched her face slightly. "Hmm, there goes my cover story then. Ho, ho." She itched her chin. "Well … um …"

"Mother, if you're going to lie to me, why don't you come out with something a bit more believable than … than Bobby! Because, let's face it, he's black. I'm almost anaemic. He's got hair quite unlike mine. I'm not going to say the word because I don't like it. Only because I think it's derogatory."

Sam Jones cocked her head. "You're speaking in rather short sentences, darling, almost as if you're tense and upset about something."

"I am tense! I am upset! My dad isn't my dad! I am, at the moment, half an orphan. And this orphan part of me wants to know who the *hell* injected his sperm into your body and made me!"

Mrs Jones raised her eyebrows. "Well, well. Aren't we the bug that turned."

"Worm."

"Hmm." Long fingernails tapped against her mother's pointy chin. "Hmm." A little pause, then: "Hmm."

"Will you stop saying 'hmm' and just tell me? I'm getting awfully bored just sitting here. Besides, when *am* I getting out of this place?"

"Tomorrow morning, in time for school, sweetheart. Don't you want you missing one of your highly important *Chemistry* lessons."

There was something particularly odd in the way that her mother stressed the word 'chemistry', almost as if it had relevance in what they had been previously talking about. And, also, what was even more odd, of course, was the fact that her mother thought that Chemistry lessons were important. Chemistry was not 'life'. People just didn't *live* for Chemistry. Ha, so there.

"Mother?"

Sam Jones's expression seemed to have been frozen into one position.

"Hold on - you are my mother, aren't you?"

"Of course. Don't be a doofus." The headmistress - as that was what she was - chuckled. "Ho, ho. Then you'll have a *complete* breakdown. Ho, ho!"

Sarah sighed and lay back on the bed.

"So … you know when you were saying about taking this girl in my mother's study?" Tony asked, sitting in the hospital café with Ben Dover, who was, for some reason, waiting in the building.

The I.T. technician sipped at his tea. He was rather sexy, for a teaching 'assistant'. Then again, that thought came from Dr Matthews, who was also waiting in the hospital so that he could see … well, so that he could waste his time, really. It was a Sunday afternoon, and raining. What else was there to do, apart from wander around and have sex? Apart from Helen Moore, Russ's sex-pal, hadn't spoken to him in several days.

Anyway, back to Ben Dover. He was tall, dark, handsome. Slim, blue eyes. A typical heroic figure in a cheap novel, but with double the strength of libido than Casanova. Russ licked his dry lips, wanting to hear that the person he *tupped* in Mrs Jones's office was a guy.

But he wasn't gay. Dover, of course. Why would Russ be even considering himself in the homosexual stakes? Whilst Ben Dover chuckled and blushed to himself, considering an answer to Andrew 'Tony' Jones's question, Dr Matthews was allowed to continue his thoughts.

Thinking about being gay now, Dr Matthews pondered what he was going to do about his sister's opportunity to ruin him. How was she possibly going to do it? And why? *For fun*, she had remarked. Fun? It was inhumane torture. As a light switched on in his brain, he grinned, "She can't prove they were my magazines!"

Tony and Mr Dover looked over at the Chemistry teacher. "Hello?" Tony asked.

"Sorry, just talking out loud. Um … anyway, what were you saying, Mr Dover?"

Ben laughed. "We're out of school now, Russ. You can call me Ben."

Tony turned to his old teacher. "Anyway, what are you here for, Dr Matthews? Russ, sorry. What are you visiting Sarah for? It's not like she's related to you or anything," he added with a slight smirk.

"Maybe I just care for my pupils," Russ replied, touching his checked shirt on the chest area.

"This is my sister we're talking about. Sarah. Jones. You two hate each other."

Dr Matthews chuckled and shook his head. "Get off it. That's like first-year behaviour. She might hate me, but I don't hate any of my pupils. I don't hold a grudge. I'm rather annoyed, actually, that you'd think that I'd form any kind of dislike for anybody."

Ben shook his head. "You're sounding like a born-again Catholic or something. These Catholics, tsk!"

Tony leaned closer to the teacher across the plastic and faintly mouldy table. "But what about all the times she's made you have accidents in the Chem lab?"

Dr Matthews growled and gritted his teeth. "Well," he said in a mean voice, a little like the stereotypical villain in action movies, "there is that."

"On numerous occasions."

"Yes, on numerous occasions."

Tony saw the cloud cover his old teacher's face and said quickly, "But, hey, that's all forgotten now, isn't it? Sarah's ill. You can't be mad at her." *Besides, she's your daughter!* Yeah, as if he'd say that to him.

But Dr Matthews was looking at the seventeen-year-old a little bizarrely. "What did you just say? She's my *what*?"

"She's your foughter."

"My what?"

"Sorry, dyslexia. I mean. She's like … um … your eternal enemy. Like an … arch-rival. Oh, bollocks, I'm off." Tony rose and swiftly left the room. Or, at least, attempted to. It took him at least three minutes to find the exit. When he did, he met it with a loud clatter as his head reacted against the wood.

"So, Ben …"

"Dr Matthews?"

"You were talking about your love-life?"

"Ah … yes. So there we were, me and this little Catholic lass in Mrs Jones's study, and suddenly …"

… and suddenly nothing became clear to Sarah at all. She wasn't even *Sarah* anymore … she wasn't sure of her own name. On the Monday morning, she found herself being sent to school in a taxi, dressed in the casual clothes she had been wearing on the Saturday night.

When she finally arrived the school, it was as if the world had suddenly stopped turning and her life had been erased. She stepped into the common room, feeling like she were her ghost and watching life revolve around her whilst there was nothing she could do about it.

Right in front of her, in the middle of the room, was her twin sister.

Twenty-four

The Zone In Which Everything Seems Unimaginable … & Pitch Black

Through her vision-damaging anger, Sarah managed to step to the centre of the room where her carbon-copy was standing, giggling and joking, waving her hands and chatting with *her* friends. She felt like her heart had been yanked out, kicked against the side wall, then retrieved and repeatedly hit at with a chrome-tipped baseball bat. Which she would invent.

"Hey, guys," she said softly, trying to break into the conversation as merrily as possible even though her head was still aching. "Hello?"

Their conversation must have not been that important - or so Sarah wished - because they turned to face her and all of their faces broke into grins. *Oh, please say this another one of my weird dreams. Please. I'd even let Tony come up and kiss … no, I wouldn't. Dammit.*

Talullaah, who was in school early for a change - even though it was break-time, close to half ten - clasped her hands together. "Oh, oh! You must be Maggie, Sarah's sister!"

Oh, sweet Jesus.

She knew it was going to happen, no doubt because she was living in some kind of a *Twilight Zone* and life just *went* like that. But even as if uncurled before her eyes, like opening a present for her birthday which she really knew she didn't want, Sarah felt herself sinking into oily quicksand, the black shit sticking to her skin and choking her as she sank.

What was she supposed to do? Fight it? Or cave in?

"Don't you just hate it when someone tells you something, and then leaves you in suspense?" asked Lucy Matthews at break-time to her brother. "Like, for example, what on *earth* I did with those photocopies of your male porn?"

She was standing in front of Russ, arms folded, smiling slightly.

"Why, what did you do with them?" he questioned. "And keep your voice down. People might hear."

"Hear that you read male porn?" she said loudly. "Anyway, I've been hearing things. That's what I'm here for. I wondered whether you knew anything about it, what with her being your … pet hate and all."

He looked up at the pig. "Sarah Jones? She has a twin sister, apparently. Well, she has. I saw her. And she's joined the school. What has that got to do with me?"

Lucy shook her ugly, squat face. "I know that, stupid. You were at the hospital on Saturday and Sunday. But what I'm hearing now along the luscious green grapevine is that Sarah's daddy isn't her daddy. Do you know anything about that at all?"

Sarah sank into a seat in the middle of the common room and pondered her options. Sink, or sink with a struggle. She saw her life from now on be divided into two - living life as herself, and as some stupid bitch of a stranger whom she'd only briefly met just before ending up in hospital.

Sink, then. Sarah was seemingly too lazy.

"*Oui*," she said, looking over at the group who had formed earlier. She glanced down at something she was playing with, and gasped out loud. In her fingers, attached to her suit jacket, was an identity tag: *Maggie Jones, Visitor*.

"I'm Maggie." Was she supposed to put a French accent on? What? This wasn't a polite little game her twin was playing with her; she hadn't let her better half in on the ambivalent rules. "And this must be … must be … my sister."

In all horrors, she noticed how her dear friend and lesser-known surnamed Tom had his pansy-arsed arm in link with her twin's chuckling heartily. "You mean you two haven't met yet?"

Sarah narrowed her eyes, "Briefly."

Maggie was wearing a dark blue suit, which Talullaah was drooling over. Sarah noticed how her twin kept having to brush away strands of saliva. "Yes," Maggie mentioned in a beautiful imitation of Sarah's non-descript accent. "I'm afraid I fell down and fainted. Stupid really."

Sarah brimmed with anger. But her French counterpart hadn't finished yet.

"I thought I was ill all day Saturday. Must have been my periods, tsk! I'm a bit of weakling, really."

Chuckling and guffawing throughout the group. Didn't people realise how odd this was? 'Sarah' was being amusing? Eerie, wasn't it? Before her twin could continue, Sarah glanced down at the badge she had been given this morning - and wondered *when* she had been given it this morning. She couldn't quite remember.

Luckily, her twin wasn't in all her lessons. In Chemistry, Sarah managed to regain her identity, much to her friends confusion. She had yanked off the identity label, shoved it in her pocket, and faced the lesson with Jenna pestering her about her change of clothing.

It seemed that only Dr Matthews was clueless about what had happened recently. At the end of the lesson, Sarah tried to chide him as best as possible, but he seemed a little flustered.

"What's up, Dr M?"

Russ Matthews rubbed off the black markings he had made on the white board that lesson, and then proceeded in trying to remove the writing. He'd been experimenting with lithium at the front of the room - enough said.

"Sorry, Sarah?"

She shook her head, flabbergasted. "Wow. You got my name right."

"Have you got a problem with your homework?"

"Well, yes. I was in hospital over the weekend, so I haven't been able to do it."

He turned, finally, lab coat awry. "That's no excuse."

"It is. I even asked my brother to bring me my homework to the hospital yesterday but he ended up handing me a book about sexual perversion and sodomy."

"What's that got to do with chemistry? Something to do with his dyslexia?"

"No, no. Tony just thought it would be a more interesting read for me." She tapped her fingers against the wooden desk. "You were a bit quiet today, Dr Matthews. Is it anything to do with the - your - male porn that your sister's been flogging around the school? If it is, there's no need to worry. My mother knows all about it anyway."

"And what did she say?"

"She asked what an anal stimulator was, and why her boyfriend Bobby wanted to use one on her."

"Oh." He added, "Any word about your father? His whereabouts?"

"No idea. How do you know about that?"

"I have no idea."

Sarah remarked bitterly, "He's not my bloody father, anyway."

With that, she stomped out of the room, attempting to slam the magnetic door behind her.

Twenty-five

Hitting That Brick Wall Already …

'Twas the hour of one, and all was silent … even Sarah Jones. And she was not in any way like a mouse. Besides, it wasn't close to Christmas. 'Twas the 24th October, the year unknown. If you have no idea in what direction I'm going in - stop reading. Go recreate your childhood.

Naturally, it was lunch-time, chewing time, and the afore mentioned Miss Jones was in the same confusing conundrum as she had been that morning. No, confusing didn't even cut it. Frustrating, more like. As she picked at her chicken and salad sandwich in the common room, seated next to Tom (who seemed to have taken a liking to her), she wanted the walls to enclose around her and allow her to be crushed between them.

"So, Maggie. What's France like nowadays? I hear they shot a lot of people," asked Talullaah. Looking at her across the table, Sarah realised just how beautiful her friend was. "We went on a school trip there donkey's years ago. Managed to get my first shipment of crack from there." She nudged her nose. "But no-one's told you anything, okay?"

"France is … interesting." Sarah had no idea. When she'd been in the second year of high school, she'd been sleeping for most of the time.

"Where abouts did you stay?" the Muslim girl asked her, taking a bite out of her cheese baguette - in rather a dainty manner, I must add.

"Oh …" Oh, bollocks. She had more chance of naming one of Talullaah's nipples than a place in France. "The North."

Maggie, who was seated at the end of the table pretending to be listening but dozing off into space, suddenly cottoned on to the fact that she could spoil a perfectly good conversation. "My mum told me you lived in Paris."

Sarah narrowed her beady eyes. "Yeah, well, *your* mother - *our* mother - tells me a lot of lies. She told me that you … that … that you fancy Dr Matthews."

Maggie giggled. "Well, I do. But that's seemingly a problem, because … hum … he's been giving it to Mummy dearest for the past twelve months."

Sarah inhaled, not knowing whether she was faking it for effect, or whether she actually believed this *cretin*. "You lie." She scraped her chair back purposely as she got up. "Maggie - Sarah, whatever the fuck your name is. Over here, please. A word."

When the two twins were together, Sarah immediately grabbed her sister's arm in the corner of the common room - the pale yellow side, with the peeling paint. "What the *fuck* are you doing? Messing up my life, eh? What's with the game?"

Maggie broke into a grin. "Fun. It helps that you've got the fashion sense of a Frenchie, as well. Besides, you might as well have fun too. There's not a lot you can do about this … predicament."

Maggie began to step away, but her sister grabbed her again. Heavy breathing, then: "*What*?"

"How come you speak with a British accent when you've been living in frog country for twelve years?"

"Good luck, I suppose."

Sarah slammed her way into her mother's study, irate. "Mother!"

"Yes, honey-bunch?"

"Don't bloody honey-bunch me." She folded her arms and did her best to look homicidal. "What's going on? Why have I been given a different identity? Why is *she* trying to make me go mad? Why, why?"

"Nobody's trying to make you do anything, darling. It's just the drugs they put you on. You must be hallucinating."

Sarah focused on the room. In front of her sat eleven strangers and her mother, placed around the main desk so that they could debate. Debate about what? *Was* she hallucinating? "So … there aren't eleven people in front of me? And you? Which would make … twelve?"

Her mother paused. "Yes, darling. But we're in a board meeting at the moment about your sister. Whether she would be allowed to continue her studies here for a while."

"No! No! You can't do that!" Sarah began to fret. "Mother, you don't know what you're doing! She's trying to ruin my life!"

The eleven members of the board sat forward, interested, as Sarah felt her feet glued to the red carpet. She looked down, shifting her feet, and found that indeed they *had* been glued - or at least, something extremely sticky was clutching at them like there was no tomorrow. "Mother, what the hell is this on the floor here?"

"Oh -" Mrs Jones rose, peeked over the heads of the other people, and laughed a little. "That must belong to David. I have no idea what it is."

"Well, it's not crap or piss, so what is it?"

"Sarah! Do *not* use language like that in front of the governors!" She turned to a gentleman with greying hair and big penis, "Sorry, she has got a rather disgusting mouth. I've warned her about it many a time."

"Where is your dog, anyway?"

"David? He's around, somewhere."

"Oh. Um … well - what are you going to do about Maggie?"

Her mother shrugged and sat down. "Shoot her?"

Sarah groaned. "She's pretending she's me in order to win my friends and say nasty stuff about me."

Mrs Jones sighed. "Life is a game of ping-pong, darling. Or, as the proles call it, table tennis."

Sarah leaned her head inward so that her mother could make a point. "And?"

"Nothing, sweetheart. Go on, then. Hop off. Enjoy the last of your lunch-time."

Twenty-six

As Much As You'd Like To Believe Otherwise, The Clock Has No Significance

Hmm, indeed. When Sarah arrived home that evening, the clock was striking five and only because her brother was hitting it with some form of a hammer. "What the hell are you doing?"

"Fixing it."

"The clock? Why?"

Her brother, who was kneeling up on the kitchen side looking set to play a court jester, lifted the wall-clock down and shook it about. "It's not broken. But it should be. The ticking irritates me. Anyway, how was your non-first day at school?"

Sarah threw her bag to the floor and kicked off her shoes. "Er, crap. My darling twin sister came into school and pretended to be me all day. Therefore, I have no friends now and thus am a loner."

Tony scratched his head. "That doesn't make a lot of sense. You'd have thought that they'd want Maggie to feel welcome, what with her being new."

Sarah frowned. "No. They don't like newness, don't my friends. They talked to me, all right. But … God! Anyway, where's the bitch staying? Hotel again? Using up some more of mother's precious money?" Suddenly, she realised that she hadn't spoken to her brother in quite some time since her fall on Saturday, and recalled the dream she had had. She blushed a little. "Um …"

"What's up?" He swiftly jumped - or crouched, then inched himself - down from the kitchen side and wiped his backside in case he'd sat in something edible.

"Nothing. I just … had a weird dream the other night. Morning. You know on Saturday when I knocked my head …?"

"Yeah?"

He looked at her, concerned, and she looked into his eyes. They weren't as similar to hers as she'd imagined, but that didn't mean a thing. The only similarity they had was that their hair was jet black. He had no other facial features equal to hers, but fuck biology.

"Nothing. It was just strange. Well, first … um … first someone told me that my dad wasn't my dad. And then … mum visited me in hospital and told me that he *isn't.* So that came true. And then …"

"And then?"

She blushed further, remembering her brother pushing her up against the wall and kissing her. And her being turned on by it all. Oh, sweet Jesus. "And then I was with you. You started … urgh … I really must have been on some killer drugs." She shook her head simply and turned away.

Tony touched her arm. "What happened?"

Sarah looked up at her brother. "You were doing dodgy rude stuff to me. Kissing me. Urgh. That is just the height of incestuous disgustingness. Urgh."

He just laughed and walked out of the kitchen with his clock, which had thankfully stopped ticking.

Hannah was crying upstairs. Tony hadn't even spotted her coming in, so he dropped the clock as hard as possible on the floor on purpose - in shock, of course - causing it to break, the face smashing into pieces of cheap broken plastic.

"Hannah, what's up?"

She was sitting on his bed, a brown envelope in her hands which had been ripped open at the top. She proffered the envelope into his skinny hands. "Read this."

He passed her it back. "Read it to me."

Hannah nodded, sniffed, and yanked out a few sheets of paper out. She scanned the pages. "It's from my parents, my family." She snuffled again. "Indirectly, of course. From their solicitors, which they didn't even bloody have until last week. Bastard solicitors." Ho, ho. "It says: blahblahblah, shit, crap, bollocks, we want to divorce you darling daughter because you are such an overwhelming burden to our family, what with you hiding in your room all the time and hardly talking."

"It really says that?"

"Read it."

Tony jumped onto the bed. He peeped over her shoulder. "'Blahblahblah, shit, crap, bollocks …' Wow, it does say that. I thought you were just summarising in a comical manner." He conceived the situation. "Oh, bloody bollocks." He turned her around so that he could look at her. "What happens? When they divorce you?"

"I have no family. I'm under eighteen, so I'll get put into care. Christ, they can do anything nowadays. Bring back the monarchy. They'd have something to say about it."

"The monarchy still exists," he pointed out slowly.

"Really? I could hardly tell." She added, "So I get put into care. Go to another school. Unless a family adopts me."

Tony put a hand to his chin and began to tap his fingers.

At the dinner table that night, around seven, Sarah cleared the plates away before her mother had finished. "I just think you want me to kill myself. Then what would you do?"

Her mother, fork in her mouth, looked up at her daughter, who was standing over her. "Hmm?" An expression of her face, Sam Jones swallowed her mouthful - without the fork, of course. "What?"

"What would you do, eh? If I killed myself? Eh? Would you feel guilty?"

"Why?"

"What would you do?" Sarah repeated, eyebrows scrunched.

Tony cleared his throat. "She'd probably adopt again, wouldn't you, Mum?" He grinned. "And I know the perfect candidate. So - go on, Sarah. Top yourself."

Hannah groaned.

Sarah dropped the plates in the kitchen sink. Her mother winced as the sound of broken crockery filled the air. "What's brought this on?"

Her daughter folded her arms when she moved back into the dining room. "I want to know about my father. Right now. Who he is. If he's dead. What he feels about being buried alive. Whether he was a good quick shag before you got rid of him and married someone else!"

Sarah's mother's eyes appeared to be popping out of her head.

"Ex*cuse* me?" asked the now hungry-ing mother of the house.

"Sorry if you're so perfect that you never let out a curse and you're so dense you think a pimp is a 'cushtie' name for a spot!" Sarah proclaimed. "And I know that decade in which I was conceived was so obviously full of sex, drugs and Barry Manilow -"

"Hey!" Tony exclaimed, easily offended at the sound of his 'idol's' name.

"- because you can't remember who my bastard arse of a father is!"

"Oh, I can, darling. I just don't think you're mature enough to appreciate who he is."

Sarah just looked at her mother for what felt like about six minutes. Her mother averted her gaze and shifted her eyes to the dining room table. "I won't tell you … because I'm … ashamed. I was five years older than him."

Her daughter made a quick calculation in her head. "So he's, what? Thirty-two, three?"

"Yes."

"Do I know him?"

"Yes."

Sarah frowned. In exasperation, she cried out: "*Bobby*?"

Her mother rolled her eyes. "Don't be ridiculous, sweetheart. Bobby's black!"

Twenty-seven

Finally …

With all her strength, Sarah smacked her mother across the face. Nobody in the room actually believed that she'd swung out. But finally, someone in this story so far did something that made sense, acting out on their own emotions. Yet that is rather too obvious.

Unfortunately, her mother didn't fall off the chair as Sarah had expected and wished her to. The older raven-haired one just jerked back a little, and then reached up to her cheek.

"Who's my bloody father?"

Sam Jones got up and walked out of the room.

A little, red-head of a voice piped up: "Dr Matthews."

Dr Matthews, on that unrevealing Monday evening, was sitting on his sofa alone. His sister had buggered off somewhere, he wasn't too sure where. He was girlfriend-less. And boyfriend-less, also, but that was beside the point.

He tapped his fingers on the salmon coloured settee, wondering whether he should mark any of the mountains of homework he had. Bollocks to it; he had other things to worry about. Like those bloody gay porn pictures. Had they really been passed around the school? Had he just imagined them stapled to the notice boards dotted around the seemingly gigantic Grammar School? Had he also just envisioned that a particular student (nameless at the moment) had added his photo on one of the pictures by computer and now *he* was the star of *Hard and Horny*?

He sighed. Things couldn't get any worse.

The phone rang.

Sarah held the phone to her ear, waiting for him to pick up. When he did, his voice sounded oddly muffled like he'd been masturbating under the duvet.

"Andrew?"

"Hello?"

"It's Sarah. Um … I need someone to talk to … can we meet somewhere?"

The afore mentioned Mr Cage chuckled. "It's seven, Sarah. What's the matter? Hey, did you like what I did to you this lunch-time? You didn't complain, anyway." Another infectious chuckle.

"Yeah, yeah, it was great," she replied, hoping it hadn't involved sodomy. "Meet me in the High Street in half an hour."

The Chemistry teacher picked up the phone.

"Y'ello?"

Sniffs and sobs. Snorts and more crying. Then: "You *bastard*!"

Oh. Helen.

"*Bastardo! Merde-tête! Scheisskopf!*"

He exhaled again. "Why are you swearing at me in foreign languages? It's not like I'd understand what they'd mean. Hang on … how do I know you're swearing, then? Perhaps it's the way your saliva is dripping out of the receiver." He wiped the handset.

"Why the *hell* didn't you tell me *what* you *were*?" The way she used the 'profanity' seemed as if she had said *fuck* or *cunting-arse-licking-twattiness.* Venom oozed from every word that came out of her mouth.

"Huh?"

"You're a bloody pufter! Aren't you! Aren't you!"

It wasn't a question. It was a statement, an accusation that needed no answering. "What?"

"I've seen those pictures. Those dirty magazines. Receipts. Lubrication specifically for anal penetration."

He had no idea about the latter item, but he was sure Lucy had cooked that up from somewhere. "There's a simple explanation for all of this, Helen."

"You tell me, you *tell me*, that you're not attracted to men at all! Go on! Go on! Just bloody prove it!"

"How can I prove it when you're not here? Come here, now, and I'll show you I don't have a thing for men." He spluttered laughter. "Fancy men! Ha, ha. Funny. It was just - er - someone - having a laugh, obviously." Russ was about to reveal his sister's identity, but due to his stupidity and loyalty to Lucy, he realised she'd been in lots of porn-y trouble if he did.

"So you want me to come over to yours, just so you can get a bloody erection? I'd be *insulted*." With that, Helen Moore slammed down the phone.

True to his word - or not (Sarah had blackmailed him with anal sex) - Andrew turned up outside the main supermarket in thirty minutes time, eyes glittering with wide impurity.

"Two things."

Andrew Cage couldn't get any words out as Sarah figuratively pounced upon him. "Bur -"

"Firstly, that was my twin sister who was pretending to be me today. She keeps doing it. To try and wreck my life."

He laughed, and swept a hand through his still long hair. "I know it was. I was just having a joke with you. I think I can tell the difference between you and Maggie. For a start, Maggie thinks that hydrocarbons are a breakfast cereal for athletes. Another thing … you're more beautiful than that frog."

"We're identical."

"Oh. She has a French sense about her, though. She smells, too."

"That's my perfume my mum gave her."

"I mean of sweat," Andrew proclaimed. "Like all good Europeans. What was your other problem?"

Sarah began to tell him, but stopped. "How come, if you knew it was Maggie, why did you talk to her all day? And ignore me?"

"Well, I had to assess her first. Form an opinion. Besides, you weren't in in the morning. You came in late today."

Sarah bowed her head. "Oh."

He nudged her arm. "How are you, anyway? Are you feeling any better? When I came on Saturday," he said with a grin, tucking back his jet black hair again, "you didn't even notice I was there. You were all yellow and shaky."

"I'm fine. Well, no. I'm not." She pointed towards a bench, which just so happened to be in front of them. "Let's stereotypically go sit down over here while I morosely tell you of my problems." They sat, and Sarah exhaled one hell of a sigh.

"What's up?"

"It's my father, who isn't my father. Well, he's run away from home. Probably because he couldn't stand to be left out anymore. Apparently, Tony isn't my brother."

Andrew folded his arms. "Well, everyone knows that."

"Huh?" She felt a tsunami of doom gush over her. Then, rain.

It pissed it down, rushing through her jumper which was streaked with white paint for no particular reason, soaking her very skin out of which she wished she could crawl.

"He's adopted," he replied, stealing her line.

"What?" Sarah asked. "How did you know?" She added, "Never mind. Everyone knew about my mum's affair and divorce, anyway, ten *years* before me." Continuing, Sarah stated, "And apparently now my real father is Dr Matthews."

Andrew slapped a hand to his forehead. "That's too unbelievable. I'd believe it if it were that Bobby lad, the one your mum's shagging. You know, he was there on Saturday. Not that you would have noticed much, being on the kitchen floor a lot." He sucked at his bottom lip. "Then again … life is shit. And unbelievable. And I believe you more than anyone. But … have you ever considered the fact that Dr Matthews is as bent as a lot of those five-quid notes several years ago?"

She shook her head. "He's camp, but not gay."

"Haven't you seen the photos of him? On the school notice boards?" He raised his dark brows. He looked a ridiculously handsome state, rain dripping from his nose and running down the little cliff underneath it. "I hear he was in a gay porn movie."

"Was that before or after he shagged my mother?" Sarah shook her hair out of her face. "I just don't believe it. Any of it. But I do. Argh! What can I do, Andrew?"

Twenty-eight

See Below

"She really likes it from behind."

Tuesday morning, staff-room, coffees steaming. Nobody seemed to drink tea in there - or at least that's what it seemed like to an edgy Russ Matthews, who was anxiously listening to Ben Dover, the I.T. technician, reveal things about his sex life.

Phh! Sex life? Dear Dr Matthews had forgotten what one was. He felt like tonight he should just go out and pull the first person that came across his path in the Local. He focused his eyes on the handsome young man in front of him.

"The young ones *are* the best," Mr Miller nodded, agreeing. "But where did you say you took her?"

"Oh - in the normal hole," replied Ben, misunderstanding. Was it Russ's imagination, or did the young lad look over at him with a secret smile? No. Surely not. "I didn't take her up the arsehole."

"No, no." The non addicted drug-addict Mr Miller, who had weaned off heroin for a good few days, grinned slightly. "I mean, in what place? Room? Did you say … Mrs Jones's *study*?"

"Yes, Iain." Ben Dover smirked. "Luckily, it was after school hours, and Marie could scream out as loud as she wanted to."

Dr Matthews peered at the I.T. technician. He was so damn sexy. Like a younger him, he supposed. Damn sexy! That's why he felt so newly attracted to the lad. He licked his lips, mouth dry, feeling himself getting hard. Shit!

Russ crossed his legs, hoping in the staff-room's bad light that nobody could see his obvious erection, protruding against restricting trousers. Did this mean … was he gay? No. No way. There just had to be something missing out his life, that was all. *Yeah, a fucking cock up your arse.*

He touched his tie apprehensively, hoping to God, which he didn't believe in, that no one looked down. So he spoke. "Well …" he blushed, feeling the attention rammed towards him like a breeze-block wall, him standing weakly behind the other side of it. "… well … I just think you should be careful, Ben. Mrs Jones found some semen on the sofa. Thought it was the dog's."

The two other men exchanged looks. "She's got a what now?" Mr Miller asked.

"A dog."

"What?" Iain asked, itching his suitcases under his eyes. "Since when?"

"Let me just get my diary out." He reached down, eyes following him. He knew what was coming even before he heard the words.

It came from the younger man. "Do you often have that erection - I mean reaction - to talk of dogs?"

For a moment, once Russ sat himself up, he couldn't speak. Then he awkwardly found his voice. "Marie? Marie Barker?"

Twenty-nine

Psychology

So, consequently, Andrew Cage didn't know what Sarah should do. She had moped around all Monday night, unsure of what to make of her life. Now it was Tuesday. The days were trickling along like sweet honey dribbling down an inner thigh, perhaps one of Andrew's. Sarah cast aside thoughts of licking the honey off by shutting her eyes in her Chemistry lesson.

Dr Matthews - her *father*, dammit - noticed what could only be perceived as her ignorance, and called on her in class. "Have you been listening, Miss Jones? You seem to be way off with the fairies!" he commented, his camp tones soaking through his words.

You can't be my father ... you're gay. She looked up, head spinning. "Um … I … I need to go to the toilet …" Sarah got up slowly, moving her stool away from her backside as carefully as possible. She stepped out of the classroom, feeling the eyes of her friends - and others - following her.

Jenna didn't rush out like the best friend that she was. No. Instead, it was the member of staff who slammed his way into the ladies' toilets like a super-hero, his tie awry and hair … well, *bent* out of shape. She was mildly surprised, but splashed cold tap water on her already pale face for comfort.

"I know you think we're … 'enemies' or something," Dr Matthews mentioned, doing bunny fingers like a Canadian, "but that's really not the case." He giggled to lighten the mood, but it didn't really help her dizziness. Instead, it still made her feel like she was going to scream out at him.

But scream what? Did she honestly believe that this *stranger* - in a personal sense - was her biological father? Could she - did she - want to accept her mother's words? More specifically … did Sarah actually realise that they weren't her mother's words, but Hannah's?

No, what she was about to ponder, was whether her so-called father knew about one of his missing sperm. And that she was standing right in front of him, shaking like a pine-cone that had just fallen from a twelve-foot tree. Possibly not quite as brown.

"Sarah?"

Officially How To Get a Man's Attention: #1 - Cry. #2 - Hit him. #3 - Throw water on him. How To Get a Man's Attention Sarah's Way: Piss yourself.

"David? Daaaaavid?"

Sam Jones was bending over the sofa when someone knocked and entered. Annoyingly, it was Mr Burch. The headmistress hadn't yet understood what his purpose in the school was, but she presumed that because he had studied Psychology, he was attempting to stop the many suicidal teenagers from killing themselves. At the moment he was winning on a ratio of 9:1.

Sam looked up from her position. "Have you seen my doggy? He's called Daavvid."

He shook his head. "No, Mrs Jones. Um … I wondered if I could ask you a favour … well, not a favour. I wanted to talk to you about your son, Tony."

"Tony? I don't have a son called that! Andrew, maybe, but not Tony! Ho, ho! Who'd want to name their son Tony?"

"Actually," he replied, sitting himself down as the head straightened herself up and brushed herself down, "I think they name their sons Anthony."

Sam shrugged. "So. What is it about my Andrew that you want to know?"

Mr 'silent H' Burch itched his little quiff. "I know a lot about … can we call him Tony, please? Andrew makes me think of that gay lad in your daughter's -

daughters's - year. Cage. Andrew Cage." He added, "Anyway … I already know quite a fair bit about your son."

"He's not my son."

"*Right*, well, that's where I was going to begin. He's adopted, isn't he?"

"Yes."

"Why did you keep that from his sister? Just like you kept Sarah in the pitch black about her twin?"

Sam Jones sniffed. That was all. Then she tossed her hair aside. Mr Burch wondered whether she was going to go into a song-and-dance routine to entwine with her histrionic nature.

"Mrs Jones?"

"That's not to be discussed."

"Okay. Then I thought I'd tell you this: I've been putting a lot of notion into your … Tony's … dyslexia, and I've come to the conclusion that he's not actually dyslexic."

"But he is! That lovely Science teacher Mr Miller tested him. And Andrew failed all of his exams." Her bright little eyes widened as she protested her case.

Burch shook his head. "Nope. I think this so-called 'dyslexia' that Tony has doesn't exist. It stems from his adoption. Wanting to be loved. Wanting attention. How old was he when you adopted him?"

"Zero."

"Excuse me?"

"He was a baby."

"How old?"

Mrs Jones shook her head. "I don't know. They all look the same to me. He was small, with a tuft of dark hair. No teeth. Plenty of saliva. And green faeces." She ran a tensely clenched half-fist through her shoulder-length hair.

"Did you already have the twins?"

"I can't remember!"

"No offence, Mrs Jones, but I think you're subconsciously hiding the past because something terrible happened then. Like who the father of the twins is."

She gnarled at her fist. "Yes, I already had the twins!"

"Why did you adopt another kid if you couldn't cope with the two you had?"

Sam Jones stood brusquely. "What is this, a bloody episode of one of those shows that even *I* can't think of the name of?? … and far too many 'of's." She sunk back into her chair, exhausted with fury.

"I'm only trying to help."

"Tell Dr Matthews that."

"What?"

"Nothing. That was the end of my sentence. Sorry? Should my words have been in italics? Tell Dr Matthews *that*," she stressed, stressing.

"Mrs Jones, breathe. Now … what about him?"

She sniffed again. "He was so good. So good in bed. Pity he's turned into a gigantic great big pufter after sixteen years."

Thirty

The Evening Comes To A Head (Sorry, Couldn't Resist)

Tuesday evening was full of mixed feelings for Sarah Jones:

"You stupid cow! I can't believe you made me bloody pee myself right in front of Dr Matthews!" Irate, she stood in front of her mother whilst the elder of the pair tried to boil an egg without the gas on. "It was *so* humiliating!" She added, "I don't know when I've been more humiliated. Oh, I know. When you became headmistress of *my* school."

"That was only a fortnight ago," pointed out her brother, who was coincidentally standing by the calendar at the front door.

Mrs Jones's bottom lip was quivering as the words that Sarah had said sunk in. She swallowed a little - saliva, not lip - and ignored the insulting statement.

"I pissed myself, mother! Pissed all over the bathroom floor."

Her mother turned around sharply. "Don't *ever* use language like that *again* in *this* household!"

"Let's face it," Tony mumbled, scratching his head as he often did, "we don't have much of a household around here."

"Piss piss piss piss piss piss," Sarah remarked, and stamped out of the kitchen.

A few minutes after Sarah had stormed away, Sam Jones burst into tears, leaning over the gas hobs, her shoulder wracking. Tony moved up behind her and put an arm around her.

"What's the matter, Mum?" he asked, showing unusual concern, but then realising that Hannah was upstairs waiting for him with a can of edible body paint and wanting to speed up the process of aide.

"I just don't know what to do …"

"Why not go see Sarah and tell her everything, about me, about Dr Matthews, about … everything?"

His mother looked up. "I didn't mean that. I meant about this egg. It just won't boil! I don't know what to do!"

Back in the future, five minutes later, Tony bounded up the stairs like a pregnant gazelle and shifted his light weight into his bedroom. Hannah was asleep. She'd fallen straight asleep in her normal clothes, bless her. She must be exhausted. Tony decided to wake her up.

"Hannah, darling … wake up. It's time for some sweet loving …"

She rolled over, muttering, "Piss off, Tony, I'm tired."

"But I want a blow job."

Hannah sat up, eyes heavy, and messed with her red hair. "What?"

He sucked his bottom lip, then went on, "We've been going out for nearly two months now. It's legally time for you to suck my penis."

She recoiled in disgust. "I'm not doing that."

"Please?"

"Oh, fucking get it out, then,"

Rather shocked, Tony reached for his zip, but then saw Hannah's dejected expression when she saw lack of bulge at the crotch of his casual brown trousers. He went to have a look. "What, you expect me to be turned on by my mother's lack of cooking skills?"

She raised her brows but said nothing; she knew there must be some logic in his words somewhere. "I said, get your dick out."

"Are you really going to … to …"

"Suck your penis? Give you a blow job? Draw into the mouth your member?"

He began to laugh. Then he dropped his smile and unzipped himself. "It'll get hard if you suck it."

Hannah groaned. "You wake me up and expect me to put my mouth around something limp? God, are you in an all-night brothel or something?"

"Sarah would do it," he muttered.

"To you? That's disgusting! I know she's not biologi -"

"I meant to anyone. We talked about it one night. But that's besides the point."

Hannah mentioned, "That's what I'd like to see. A point. A long, hard one."

"Put your hand round it."

"I'm not touching it!"

"Then how are you expecting to suck it without touching it?"

The red-head growled. Hannah. She reached out a small hand, clenched her eyes shut, and wrapped her fingers around something hard and smooth.

"Ouch! That's my bloody leg, Hannah!"

She opened her eyes and let go. Her heart was fluttering quite stupidly. Tony had pulled his trousers down to the top of his thighs, revealing a lot of flesh and meat. She'd seen enough men's penises on the walls of her parents's bedrooms, but she'd never seen her boyfriend's. Never even imagined what it'd look like. Should it be that small?

As if reading her mind, he came out with: "Do you want a ruler? It's not even hard yet. And that's big, even … er … not hard."

Hannah sighed. With Tony sitting on the bed, she positioned herself so that she would have full range of his apparently delectable genitalia. She touched the thing with warm fingers. It was warmer than the inside of her armpit, which she was clutching onto with her other hand for support - and er, support of the morale kind.

"Um, um … hold on. I just need to go to the toilet. Wank yourself off or something. Where's that magazine of middle-aged soap-stars again?"

"What? You want it?"

She rolled her eyes and moved out of the bedroom.

Inside the Jones's bathroom, Hannah pulled her mobile phone out of her jeans pocket and dialled a number. Marie's.

When Marie picked up, Hannah could hear loud moaning and shuffling of something, like many fabrics moving in different directions. She decided it would be safe to talk.

"Marie? Marie? How do you give a blow job? Marie?"

"Just … suck … suck it hard … and deep. Get it all in. Don't stop … harder, harder …" came a male voice, presumably not Marie's unless she'd been on that reversal to helium they'd founded some time ago.

"Oh … okay," Hannah replied. "Cheers." She hung up and moved back into her - and his - bedroom.

Suck it, suck it hard. That's what Hannah had heard. She rehearsed it in her mind after she had landed herself back on the bed where a more hyperactive than normal Tony sat. He was jumping up and down on his arse like a monkey about to be injected with adrenaline in the electric chair.

"Where d'ya go, where d'ya go?" he asked.

"Oh, fuck off and pull your trousers down again," she muttered.

He did as she commanded, and immediately wanted to vomit thinking about putting that … that *thing* in her mouth. She licked her lips, quite nervous, but that seemed to turn her boyfriend on even more and she saw the … thing … become harder and even as she tried to avert her eyes, she found herself staring at it even more.

Well, come on, what are you waiting for? It's not going to stay like that all night. Just don't make it seem like you haven't done it before.

Hannah resumed the position. She grabbed his … "What do I call it?" She looked up at Tony.

"Huh?" he asked, voice breaking even though she hadn't yet placed her mouth around his instrument of pleasure and urination.

"What do I call *this*? For my inner monologue?"

"I don't know *what* you're on about. But if you'd just like to place your firm pink lips around the shaft of my …"

"I have to have a name for your … thing. Otherwise I can't concentrate."

"I don't know! John Thomas? Beef soldier? Bacon rod? Meat wrench?"

"Oh, sweet Jesus. You've been looking names up on the Internet, haven't you?"

He shook his head. "It's a man's prerogative. Love pump. Flesh rocket."

Hannah sighed. She took his …er … pump in her hand a little more tightly and then placed her mouth around it. Immediately, he let out a moan which no doubt would send Sarah and her mother running, if not for their own personal problems.

She recalled what the guy had said on the other end of Marie's phone line, and rammed as much of his meat (without veg) down her throat as possible. Not going to happen. Or, at least, Tony thought it was going to happen, and stuck his large hand on the back of her head and pushed her head down onto his dick. Right down the back of her throat.

Oh, holy mother of God. She felt the bile rushing up her throat as she choked but tried to stop it anyway. She didn't quite know when the point was when she realised that there was no way the vomit wasn't going to stay down. Perhaps just as she attempted to move against Tony's strength and get his goddamn penis out of her mouth, which was rapidly filling with sick.

Maybe Tony didn't just see what was happening; didn't see her flailing arms, or her face turn a hot pink. She prised his fingers away from her head, the sick splashing out now, Tony only just understanding that, oh God, she was being sick on his knob, oh God, get it away … it wasn't his fault …

Her mouth was totally free now, and she was surprised - mildly, at least - to see how little she had actually thrown up. However, without even looking at her boyfriend's expression, she jumped up and raced down the stairs, slipping into her shoes and out of the house. She entered a couple of seconds later to rinse her mouth out in the kitchen, but Tony didn't see any of it. He was too busy staring at his bacon rod, which looked a little raw.

Thirty-one

Acid + Base = Salt + Water, So I've Been Told. But Who Actually Believes Chemistry Teachers?

"So I hear you pissed yourself in front of Dr Matthews," Sarah said during break time the following morning to her twin sister, who was seemingly still posing as … er, the respected pissée.

Talullaah began to snicker behind a hand. "Maggie, that's what I like about you! You're so … vibrant!"

Five of them were sitting on apparently 'comfortable' chairs in their common room during the hour of ten. Jenna and Tom - who were kissing despite the fact that he was still dusting the cobwebs out of the closet - and Talullaah, Sarah and Maggie. Or Maggie and Sarah. Whichever way you looked at it.

Maggie went pink. "Um …"

Talullaah brought out a lollipop from out of her Versace bag and started to open it and suck at it. "Has anyone heard from Hannah today? She was supposed to be in today. We had a presentation to do." When nobody replied (Jenna more concerned about Tom's lack of erection than anything else), the Muslim girl went on: "So, Sarah, about this pissing. Why? Pissing your pants is *so* last summer with the humongous drought etcetera."

Maggie got up, stumbled around, then snatched her twin sister away from the group. Irate, the alien sister was chewing on her lip so dreadfully that Sarah was hopeful, at least, that Maggie might chew it off, and then the two of them could be distinguishable.

"What the fuck are you doing?"

Sarah smiled. "Just having a little fun, like you were on Monday. Fun, isn't it? And do me a favour. Leave Andrew alone, would you? He can tell the difference between us, just like Tony can."

Maggie folded her arms and during speaking, Sarah could swear she heard a trace of a French accent. Then again, Sarah could swear. "Ah, ah, *mais oui*. Tony. The brother of ours who isn't actually our brother."

"Of course he's our bloody brother. Just because he was adopted … that doesn't mean bollocks. He's been my brother for … many years, and that's the way I look at him." *Despite that sick dream.*

"*Bien sûr*. But surely you look at him differently now?"

"I don't know what the hell you're getting at, you twisted little French fuck, but I'd really appreciate it, *sister*, if you'd piss off back to frog-land and not come back. And in the mean-time, start being *you*."

"*Naturellement*, Sarah."

"And stop speaking pissing French. I've had enough of that language." Sarah brushed past her sister and back to her friends.

"I've shagged Andrew Cage," Maggie started up with immediately.

Sarah hit her head with her palm.

During her forever delayed Chemistry lesson in which she often wished she had a bottle (hydrochloric acid) to drown her sorrows in (throw on her teacher), Sarah focused her attention on Dr Matthews for a change.

She hadn't looked in the mirror recently, so couldn't really decide whether she had the same facial features as her alleged father. Did he know? If he did, would he stop picking on her in class?

"Miss Jones?"

Not again. "Yes, Dr Matthews?"

"The lesson hasn't even started yet and you look like you're about to drop off."

"My stool? Or to sleep?"

"You know what I mean," he mentioned.

She was surprised that only she and Jenna were in the lab, considering the fact that they were twelve minutes late already. Then again, Dr Matthews wasn't exactly commonly accepted to be on time to any of his lessons.

"And why were you looking at me, anyway?"

"I keep getting you confused with your sister. There's not much difference between you and her, is there?"

Sarah smiled. "My hymen is intact, Dr Matthews." But her smile turned into a frown when she heard echoed in her mind what she'd just said. "Sorry. I didn't mean to be crude." She scratched her cheek, which was reddening, and glanced down to the lab bench.

"Oh, apology accepted, Miss Jones. I was just going to ask you how your bladder was, actually."

Jenna rolled her eyes, twiddled with her peach-coloured hair, but said nothing.

"Rapidly pressing against my lower genitalia as we speak."

"Would you like to use the toilet now, before the rest of the class enter?"

She didn't look up.

"Sarah? *Sa*rah? Come on, at least retort with something vaguely insulting!"

She narrowed her eyes, finally allowing herself to peer up at the teacher: "Oh, piss off."

He raised his brows. "Not bad, not bad. Don't like the foul language, but what can we do?"

"Ground me?" she suggested, hoping for some kind of hint that he knew about his daughters.

"I suppose," he replied, though, "you've only been taught by the worst. Parents, I mean."

She didn't even realise how little he knew her mother's devout hatred of swearing, because Sarah was taken aback by his dream-like comments. She had to shake herself to wonder whether she was still awake. Jenna next to her, though, was sniggering. That might have been a reaction to the hair-dye.

"Oh, I'm sorry, Miss Jones. Didn't mean to be so crude."

Did he know? She doubted it.

"I wouldn't insult me, Dr Matthews. I know things about you that *you* can't even remember." She added as an afterthought, "Literally."

The hour-long lesson passed by without another irritable comment from either of the two sides, both bitterly sober and narrow-mindedly angry about their stale-mate situation.

At the end of the lesson, as always and *unintentionally*, Sarah stayed latest knowing she didn't have to slope hurriedly off to her next lesson; she had free periods. Jenna rushed away, the best friend that she was, leaving Sarah accidentally alone in the lab with Dr Matthews. Had they not been doing only theory that day, she would have been petrified at what chemicals he had to hand that he might throw at her. Accidentally, of course. He was a prat, but his spillages were not always directed at her, and were never intentional.

She hoped.

"So …" he began, as she knew he would as she put her papers together, "… what's this you know about me?"

"You're acting as though you have something to hide," she replied without looking up.

"Yes, but then again, I don't involuntarily urinate in front of members of staff, do I?"

She blushed and refused to look up.

"Sarah?"

"Mmm?"

"Look at me."

Later she'd reenact this scene in her head and realise how fatherly he sounded at that point. However, in the present, she just managed to inch her head up. He was standing in front of her sanded-down, spilt-on-with-acid bench, looking rather impish. Hang on, he always looked impish.

"I'm sorry if I insulted you. In front of your best friend, as well. But let's face it, she's not really your best friend. Just kind of there for show. But … um … anyway … I'm sorry."

Something wasn't right here. He was apologising. No, no … not a dream. She pinched herself. Yet didn't wake up. Interesting. "What?"

"I know I'm not the maturist of people, and you apparently hate my guts … but I am human. And it *is* six of one thing and half a dozen of the other."

Sarah sighed. "Why should it be? You're a teacher, for God's sake. You *should* be more mature. And a better role-model."

He laughed. "Role-model? Me? A thirty-three year-old camp-sounding Northern man? To who? The gay population of the school? Did you *see* that *porn* they were sticking up of me all over the school?"

"Lucy was."

"Yeah, they, Lucy, whatever. I mean, everyone thinks I'm gay anyway. It doesn't help my … head when … there's all … that going on."

"I don't think you're gay," she lied, or hoped she lied. A few months back, although Dr Matthews had been humping the Languages teacher Miss Moore, Sarah had told her friends that she was convinced of his pillow-biting sexuality. Now, what with the father-thing, she wasn't so sure.

"It's not really any of your business, but thanks."

"Oh, but it is."

He seemed to pull his face wide with his expression, a make-shift face-lift. "What do you mean?"

She shook her head. "I don't … um … I have to go … go waste my time in my free period."

"Sarah … do you want to talk to me about something?"

Yes, Dr Matthews. Dad. You're my father. Remember that night you boned my mother? No, I don't even know about my conception either. Hmm, best ask my mum about that. Um ... you were very drunk and you slipped your dick into my mum's warm bits. No, not her mouth. Yes, down below. The second hole, not the third. Yes, our sex has three holes. One we piss out of, but you saw me demonstrating that yesterday, didn't you?

"Sarah? Are you okay? You seem to be mouthing something. What? Hello?" He waved his palm across her face.

"I'm fine."

"Are you sure?"

His caring attitude made her visibly shudder.

"I've got a lesson with the year above you next, but they can bugger off and do their own stuff if you want to talk."

She wanted to stay and chat with him, yet didn't feel the ultimate urge to reveal to him his surprise parentage. "Okay, okay," she replied, thoughts running through her already over-worked brain. A-level Chemistry - ouch.

"Come into my parlour, little fly," he invited, with an unearthy and horrendously camp cackle that even Sarah had to smile at. He walked down the Chemistry corridor and pushed open the I.T. room door.

Inside, neither of them could believe their eyes. Marie Barker and Mr Dover were going at it like rabbits with knowledge of the upcoming apocalypse.

Thirty-two

Repression and Pre-depression

"Er … wrong room. Let's go in the one next door." That came from Dr Matthews, who had been, for several minutes, transfixed with the in-out, in-out movements of Marie Barker, sitting astride -

"Ben Dover the I.T. technician!" the teacher cried out.

Marie, seemingly tired, turned around. "How's that going to happen? How can I get penetrated in that position?"

Dr Matthews backed out of the room, shaking a little, and shut the green door quietly behind him. Sarah, already purple with humiliation, moved swiftly to the next room.

"So, Miss Jones, what seems to be the trouble?"

"First of all, stop calling me that."

"Okay. Maggie."

She sighed.

"Joking!"

"Whatever. Anyway … I … you probably know that my father - the one who's 'brought me up', uh, fed me, and been invisible really, uh, that's about it … well, he's not my real father. I couldn't care less. He's just bugg-gone off somewhere. I don't know why. They were getting divorced anyway." She glanced down, up again, and spotted his face again. Ooof. What a face.

"Anyway … um … my mother has revealed to me who my real father is."

"I see. Not good news, is it?"

"Not really," she smiled sardonically.

He tapped his fingers on his chin, which had now become almost a cliché. "Interesting. Ironic that your *adoptive* father runs off. Usually it's the other way around: the biological father runs away for some reason, like being annoyed with his wife for having an affair with the family photographer … and leaves the poor mother to fend for herself … only to come back years later and pretend that he hasn't been away in the capital, shagging dirty little prostitutes that were ten-a-penny and fornicating with the pigeons next to that Column that was knocked down last year, the little, little, *tiny* man. Not even a man. An ant. That you could just crush," at this point, pink, Dr Matthews grinded his thumb and first finger together, "because that's just what he was, an insect. Nothing. Dead."

"Er, Dr Matthews?"

"Yes?"

"My problem?"

"Oh, yes, sorry. Anyway, I was saying … it's quite absurd … I mean, different, that your other father should run away. Um … anyway. Your real father. He abandoned you at birth, I suspect?"

"Something like that."

"Hmm. And does he know about him being a father of twins?"

"No."

"Oh."

"He's a teacher. Here. He slept with my mother sixteen years ago because he was very, very drunk at the time."

"I see," Dr Matthews. "Well … the best thing to do, Sarah, is tell the teacher. What can he do? Run off again? Well, I suppose he could. Just - listen - take it *one step at a time*."

She nodded. "Okay," she answered and got up from the old stools. "Thanks."

Sarah left the room, without seeing her teacher's expression. It was a mixture of pure horror, fear, and recognition.

Thirty-three

Toilet Trouble

Sarah barely missed the fact that Andrew was absent from school all day, simply because she remembered it was going to happen. What she was more concerned about, and concerned that she was concerned, was where Hannah was. Her brother's girlfriend was the punctual type, obsessively almost.

During two minutes in the rest of her free periods, Sarah dialled Hannah's number in the female toilets and listened to ringing. Her mobile pressed to her ear, she was worried about how she could actually hear the ringing of another phone, almost as if Hannah herself was hidden in one of the stalls. She was.

"I'm not coming home tonight," Hannah stated after the pair of them realised what was going on. They emerged from the cubicles, both looking dishevelled. "I did something so stupid last night with Tony … I mean … Last night …"

Sarah and her friend washed their faces with cold tap water. "What happened? I heard someone rush out last night, but I didn't know it was you. You were at the usual bus-stop this morning, so I presumed you'd got up extra early and … I dunno."

"Can we go sit down? I think Tony fucking hates me."

Back in the common room, empty apart from a teacher and student having an extra lesson - one of them smoking what looked like a spliff whilst the other looked up at their teacher disdainfully.

"Go on," Sarah began as they sat in the corner of the large room. "Tell me what the fuck-up was."

Hannah raced fingers through her hair, reminding the darker-haired one of herself a little. She had no idea why. "I … he asked for a blow-job."

"Eugh."

"Hmm, I know. He … said it was legal or something … he …"

"… was talking crap again?" injected the brunette.

"Yeah. How did you know?" she asked ironically. Hannah continued, "So I started to do it, get down to it, but I thought I'd ring Marie to ask for some tips."

"Good choice."

"But she sounded like she was busy."

"She's shagging the I.T. technician," Sarah recalled, reddening a little. She pushed back hair from out of her eyes.

"Anyway, to cut a long story short, he pushed my head down too far …"

"Eugh!"

"… and I … puked all over his dick."

Now Sarah found she couldn't get any words out. "Um … I'll … just ring my brother."

In the male staff toilets - oh, yes, the Grammar School had them - Mr Miller stood by the sink washing his hands and preparing a couple of lines of talcum powder to sniff, whilst waiting for his chemical colleague to exit the one of two cubicles.

"I don't know what you're shitting yourself for," Iain said, before snorting the first line of talc. He coughed, squeezed his nose, then wiped it. "That's bloody strong baby powder," he muttered, glancing up at the plastic bottle.

"What?" called Dr Matthews from the loo, rapidly pulling another metre long sheet of roll to wipe himself with.

"Nothing. I just said, I don't know why you're shitting yourself. But would you please give it a flush? It sounds like someone throwing cruise-boats down the Niagara Falls."

Russ obliged.

After another couple of minutes, he came out, (so to speak), looking a little pasty. He caught Iain snorting the other line of white powder. "Are you … snorting … *talcum powder*?"

"Yeah," Iain replied. "Apparently if I do anymore drugs then I'll die. So I'm sticking to a few mg's of smack at the week-end, and replacing the cocaine with baby powder. It's a good substitute. And bloody cheap. Want some?"

Russ shook his head vaguely. "I've never touched drugs in my life, and never will."

"Not even talcum powder?"

"Talc isn't a drug."

"So have some."

"Iain! I do not participate in any drug-taking manners! I don't even know what taking drugs feels like!"

All of a shocking sudden, Russ was transported back to almost seventeen years previously … a party … punch … plastic cup … someone brushing past him … him drinking the punch … feeling woozy … that woman coming up to him … dressed as Morticia … sexy, sexy woman … moving to her car … back seat … heavy shagging … in out in out in out … steamy windows even though the top was down … sweat … perspiration … glowing …

Russ sped into the cubicle again, locked it, and yanked down his trousers.

Thirty-four

An Incident

It was freezing in the English room that afternoon, and their second English teacher Mrs Green had a lot to say about that. That was, when she turned up, wearing barely nothing apart from a whopping great big crucifix around her neck and some kind of chiffon dress. "Surely this can't be legal!" she groaned, shivering, her bony skeleton obvious through the thin fabric. "I must report this. Right. Now. Down to business. Sarah Jones, why for *goodness*' sake didn't you hand the homework in? Why? Why?"

Ah, just another wondrous Mrs Green lesson. Full of sound and fury and all that crap. What Sarah herself didn't understand was why they were doing the same Shakespeare play with two teachers, when Marie's class were studying *Antony and Cleopatra* and a modern novel or two. So she jerked back into existence.

"Um …"

"*Um* just isn't good enough, Sarah. Hell's bells," she remarked with a tug of her short dark hair. "What do I have to do to get through to you lot? You're like little children in the Reception classes!" She added, "Well, Sarah?"

"But I've just found out I have a twin sister." Mrs Green just stared with eyes as wide as golf balls. No, that's exaggerating. More like footballs. "And … I've just come out of hospital."

"And?"

"And I've just found out that my father isn't who I thought he was."

Surely some sympathy?

"And? Sarah, I'm not interested in excuses. You get that work in to me by tomorrow morning, or else … Well … We'll just have to see. You're old enough now to recognise your priorities." The teacher sniffed. "Now. Where were we? Act three, yes, Act three. The other groups have already finished this play and have started reading *War and Peace* for fun. Time is essence, girls," (for that's what they all were - no boys insisted on taking this subject due to piss-fear of Mrs Green), "and we must move on."

Sarah searched through her bag unenthusiastically, and couldn't find the book. She could picture it in her mind. Old, scratty around the corners, page xi torn slightly. Pages xxi and xxx-iv completely ripped out. Only an introduction. Nothing important.

In fact, Sarah noticed, the book looked exceedingly (like the cakes) similar to the one Talullaah had in her smooth, tan-coloured hands. Smooth.

"Is that my *Antony and Cleo*?" she whispered to her friend.

"Yeah. Lost mine. Why?"

"Well," she pestered. "I need mine."

A voice shrieked from the front, "Sarah Jones! Not only do you disrupt my lessons at the start, but at the beginning also? Pure insolence! Absolute impertinence! Girls, you should be writing this vocab down. At the moment, your vocab skills are as simple as a five-year-old's! Actually, when my son was five, he knew what impertinence was. Probably because he was continuously setting fire to his friends's houses. Er … anyway, Sarah! What seems to be the trouble now?"

"Talullaah has my *Antony and Cleopatra*," she replied, feeling herself now like a five-year-old.

"And? Why don't you have hers?"

"Because," she spluttered, "she's lost hers! Obviously. *So* predictable."

Mrs Green folded her arms. "Well … I have *never* seen such a display of mutiny in my life before? And especially Talullaah, with her lovely, lovely, arrr, hair and all."

Sarah groaned noisily, almost an orgasm sound, and hit her head on the desk, blacking herself out. Ouch.

Thirty-five

Like Father, Like Daughter

Russell Matthews stalked past the main notice board in the school's entrance and ripped off one of the many photocopies of himself and another guy in a fairly difficult position. Clutching it in a death-like grip in his left fist, he paced to Mrs Jones's study and felt the inevitable had to be faced.

However, before he could *inevitably* step inside the gigantic glass-cabinet of the secretary's room, he was caught on the arm by none other than the Great Humper, Ben Dover. Mr Dover looked a little unkept, almost as if he had just been participating in hot sex with one of the pupils. Which was possible. His burgundy tie was at an angle, the white stripes in it vaguely missing.

"Mr Matthews …"

"Dr."

"Whatever. The thing is, er, Russ …" He ushered the teacher closer to the wall. Russ immediately wondered whether Mr Dover was going to physically proposition him and ask him to bend over. Russ would have to thank him but decline. He wasn't in that kind of thing.

"… Marie and I … um … I mean … it's not as if … it's illegal …"

Russ shook himself awake. "Of course! I caught you two having sex! We, me and Sarah. Oh God …" He clutched at his stomach and danced about on the spot for a moment, which seemed to stop the gurgling. "Hold on … that means that I have one up on you, don't I?"

"Not really. Not after you got turned on by … er … *me* in the staff-room."

"You're a bit modest aren't you?"

"Not particularly. I know I'm as handsome as a fox. Smart, good with my hands. Good at pressing all the right buttons, if you know what I mean. Hung like a fucking donkey," he lowered his voice at this point, but then raised it again. "What would *Sarah* think to you getting turned on by a guy? And this thing, here, in your hand." He wafted it a bit. "What does she think of that, eh?"

"Sarah? Which one?"

"Headmistress's daughter, you fool. There's no other Sarah in the school. Once a popular name, now … a laughing-stock."

"You're talking bollocks."

"I just might be, but I could tell her all about your homosexual cravings. She wouldn't like that, would she?" Ben asked with a wink.

"I don't have - that's disgusting! And what's Sarah got to do with anything?" he questioned, wondering if Ben knew more than he should. Or knew stuff that wasn't totally true. Or true at all. Or had *any* smidgeons of truth in them, like those things he was saying about him being 'gay'.

"Like there's nothing going on between you two. Marie and I saw the pair of you in the science lab after Sarah's lesson. Got us rather randy, if you know what I mean."

"No!"

"The spark between you two. The *Chemistry*, if you will."

"Urgh!" He made a disgusted face and felt like he was going to vomit. In fact, he raced up to the staff-room, to the toilets, found them to be in use, then sped to the public ones just down the corridor. He discovered that emptying his stomach leaning over a cracked plastic toilet seat was immensely satisfying.

At the end of the school day, Sarah went to see her mother about her impending crisis which was taking over her life. Her mother was on her knees, as she quite often was, trying to find her puppy.

"I've lost him again, darling. He was under the cabinet over there," she pointed, wafts of dark hair sliding into her face, "making poo-faces, and since then I don't know where he's gone. He has been leaving little *proofs* of himself though. Filthy little animal."

Her mother peered under the sofa. "I think he might be under there. Daaaavid? Are you therrrrre?"

"Do you know how ridiculous you look, mother?"

"Don't call me mother. It's horrible. How about Mum? Mumsy? Sam?"

"Mother! I have a problem!"

The headmistress got up and straightened herself down. "What is it? And why should I help you, anyway? You slapped me the other night. Don't think I forget things that easily."

"It's about my dad."

"Who?"

"Dr Matthews."

"Oh. That thing."

"Yes."

There was a stony silence. Mrs Jones picked up a rock of a paperweight and began throwing it from hand to hand. After a close encounter of paperweight and foot, Sam Jones decided that it would be better just to place the object on the table and fiddle with it there.

"What about -"

Sarah cut in: "Well? Does he know? Does he know he's the father of twins?"

Sam shook her head. "He was drunk. More than drunk. What do you call drunker than drunk? Rat-bottomed? Anyway … I don't like to talk about it."

Sarah's mother sat on the sofa, stood immediately upon encountering something wet and slimy, and then perched herself on the old wooden desk.

"You have to. He has a right to know. How did it happen?"

"Long story."

"Mother!"

"A party. Friend's. Mutual acquaintance. He was friends with my friend's younger brother. Something like that. I was only twenty-two, for goodness's sake! Unmarried! Didn't think I ever would! And to be totally honest, lad I was dating at the time thought that my clitoris was called a dingleberry."

"Dad? I mean, Lesley?"

"Yes."

Sarah sighed. "Carry on."

"I hadn't … scrouperized for a fairly long time."

"You hadn't *what*?"

"You know. I hadn't had a … goose and duck … in a while."

"Rhyming slang?"

"Yes."

"Mother!" Sarah blustered, "And … he got drunk? How drunk?"

"Someone must have slipped rohypnol or whatever it was in those days into his drink. He started making eyes at me first. Hilarious to watch. He tried to make his move on me. Shifted awkwardly over to me …"

"... Hey, babe. Are you that news-reader woman?"

Of course, I had nothing to do but agree with him. He was so obviously out of his head that he couldn't care less whether I was male or not. Nevertheless, he was damn sexy, gorgeous-looking. He grabbed a hold of one of my -

"Hold on," Sarah cut in, "are you sure we're talking about the same Dr Matthews here? Five-ten, skinny, camp, dark-hair, *not* sexy?"

"Everyone to their own, Sarah. Anyway …"

...He grabbed one of my glands ... with a shaking hand, and murmurred, "I know I'm not an adult yet, but if possible, I'd like to take you for as long as empirically possible in the back-seat of your car. Because I don't have one yet. But I've started lessons."

He sounded so sweet and attractive that I just had to have him. So I led him to my car, the back-seat. I had one of those convertible things in those days, and we were so drunk and hyper that we ... did it *with the top down. He liked that. People could see him.*

"You're so brilliant," he told me after the event. "Even if you're, like, five years older than me. Can we do it again?" But after realising how carried away I'd become, I pushed him out of the car - remember the top was down, so I did literally push him out. It was more of a roll, though, because he was so intoxicated.

And that's about it.

Sarah had been squirming from the very beginning when her mother had said 'babe', but now she had turned a deep beetroot colour. "You didn't have to go into so much detail. I get the idea."

"Good. Then you won't ask again." Her mother paused before adding, "Are you going home now, darling? You'll miss the bus, won't you?"

She shrugged nonchalantly. "I dunno. What is there to go home to?"

"Your brother."

"He's not my brother."

Her mother tutted and folded her arms. "There's no use having an attitude like that, Miss Jones. Otherwise you'll end up like your father. And I mean the camp Northern monkey, not the one who's brought you up."

Sarah screamed out with exasperation. "What's wrong with Dad? He's done bloody more than what Dr Matthews has done!"

"Well, he's impotent, for one thing. But he sleeps around. Interesting, isn't it, hmm?" Sam Jones tapped her fingers at the side of where she was perched. "Has faulty sperm, too, and everyone knows that. Yet how has he managed to father two - well, three - children? The miracles of Our Lord, eh?"

Sarah screwed her eyes up. "Why do you have to be so bloody cynical about stuff? And why did you drive Dad away? I didn't need to know any of this! You've ruined my life! I can never forgive you for that!"

In a huff, the girl stalked out of the office, almost taking half of the rug with her which stuck to her shoe. She slammed the door behind her and slammed straight into her father.

Thirty-six

Surprises

"Dad - what are you doing here? Where have you been all this time?"

Lesley Jones ran a hand through his dark hair and sighed noisily. "It's a hideous story." He held a brown envelope in his hand, one of those A4 jobs with the long slip of paper not peeled from the end yet to seal it. "Let's just go inside and talk with your mother."

Sarah went bright red. Or at least, a darker shade that induced embarrassment. "I can't do that. I've just angrily poured my heart out in a tearful yet irate manner. I can't go back in there." She was still a little perturbed by her father's appearance after all this time.

"Oh. Well. Go home, then. But you'll kick yourself when you miss out on everything that goes on in here."

She shrugged. "A good kicking never hurt no one."

The thing was, Sarah had promised to meet Hannah outside the school as soon as she possibly could so that they could catch the bus home together. The raven-haired one didn't quite remember that, but did so with a whack against her own forehead when Hannah grabbed her by the front gate.

"You met me, after all!"

"Oh, yeah. Sorry … had to sort out a few bits and pieces that now resemble my life."

"Oh … sorry. Is it that bad?"

"I have no …" She stopped, realising what she going to say and then correcting herself. "I found out quite recently that -" She stopped in the middle of the street; they had just started walking to the bus-stop. "Hold on, why am I telling you this? You already know all about Dr Matthews."

"Yeah."

"You were the one who blurted spontaneously that Dr Matthews was my biological father."

"Yeah," repeated Hannah, wondering where all this was heading. Down the gutter, as far as her footsteps were concerned.

"Oh." Sarah inhaled the late-October air through her lungs. It was going dark already, and she found herself staring miserably at the rotting leaves on the pavement as they slowly stumbled down the road. “So … what are we going to do about Tony, then?”

Hannah grumbled, “I don’t want to see him. But I’ve got nowhere to stay.”

“Stay at my house, then,” Sarah answered with a grin.

“It’s not funny … I don’t want to face him. Well, actually, it’s not his face I’m afraid of seeing, actually.”

Sarah scratched her head. “What ever made you want to … do … *that*, anyway? It’s such a degrading act … like you’re his slave. I’d never do that, not even to Andrew.”

“Cage?”

“Uh-huh.” Woefully she exhaled, “God, I missed him today. He seems to be the only one apart from you and Tony that makes any sense around here any more.” She snapped out of her daze. “But back to you. Tony doesn’t hold a grudge. He’s not mature like that, he doesn’t understand what one is. There’ll just be a few blushes and nervous glances and that’ll be the end of it.”

When they got home, they found that Tony had locked them out of his bedroom.

Half an hour later of pounding on the male member of the household’s door, without him giving in, Sarah finally retreated to her parents’ - or parent’s - bedroom and used the phone in there to dial direct to her mother’s study.

When her mother picked up, Sarah heard a blast of: “You evil, scheming whore of a woman!” before, “The Grammar School, how may I help you, Home?”

"Mother, it's me."

"Me?"

"Sarah. Your daughter."

She heard in the background: "Oh! Which one! There's so bloody *many* of them!"

Her mother said loudly, "What's the matter, sweetheart? Your father and I are just having a *discussion* about the divorce, etcetera etcetera."

"Yippee-dee," she heard her father exclaim sarcastically in the background.

She ignored that. "Tony's locked himself in his bedroom and won't let us in."

Mrs Jones pondered, "Perhaps he's … going *mingo*."

"What??"

"You know, darling, *playing* with himself."

Lesley Jones shouted loudly: "Masturbating, wanking, tossing off, jerking off, frigging himself. Christ, Sam, I wish you'd remove that red hot poker you've got rammed up your little arse."

Sarah cut in, "No, he's not doing *that*. He usually has the door open when he does that. For the thrill of it."

"Well, I won't be able to help you until later, darling," Sam Jones slowly, possibly aiming to delicately yank out the said instrument from her rectal area. "I don't think I'll be home until your bed-time, honey-bunch."

Her daughter exhaled. "Half eight, then?"

"Around that time, yes, darling."

"Let us in, Tony," his sister shrieked for the twentieth time that afternoon, which was swiftly turning into evening before their eyes. "This is no way to act. You're so bloody immature it's untrue." A pause. "I'll make Hannah go in my room, okay. You don't have to see her. Okay?"

She turned to Hannah. "Just go in my room for a minute until I coax him out of this … cocoon. It won't take long. I know him. I have a magic power over him. Just watch."

She ushered Tony's girlfriend into her room, which was adjacent to her brother's. After closing the door shut, Sarah tapped lightly on the polished wood. "Tony? She's gone. Let me in."

There was a click, and the handle then shifted a little. The door creaked with eerie tension. Finally, after so long, the door opened and Tony peeped his head through the thin slit of light.

Thirty-seven

No Progress

"Just talk to her, would you!"

Iain Miller was sitting in the local pub with Russ Matthews sipping at a fruit juice intoxicated with half a bottle of vodka. Or, as he had asked for it, all the vodka the bar-man could get in a pint glass, with a dash of orange.

"Who?" The answer could be several things: Helen Moore, with whom he'd had a little 'argy-bargy' (his phrasing); Mrs Jones, his wham-bam, oops-there-it-spills-ma'am single hump, or thirdly his daughter. Daughters, technically, although he more or less saw them merged into one at the moment. Just fatter.

"Who have we just been talking about?"

"We've just been talking about … um …"

Russell nursed his pint of lager miserably, then announced: "I can't remember. I wasn't really concentrating."

"Aren't you *adorable*," Mr Miller said in his best and campest Dr Matthews' voice. "You were going to tell me about Sarah Jones. About shagging her mother. About letting Sarah know that you know that she's your daughter."

The younger teacher screwed up his eyes. "I can't do it. How am I supposed to break it to her?" He took a swig of his drink. "'Hey, Sarah. That bastard of a father you were talking about is me! Yeah! Yippee! Isn't that fine and dandy! Now turn to page sixty-three in your text-book and stop bloody talking to Jenna.' I can really picture that happening."

"She might know who her father is."

"No, she doesn't. She would have told me if she knew."

Iain cocked his peppered-covered head. Almost literally, for he had been playing around with the cruets on the oak table in front of them; remnants of their 'priority-dinner' they'd had this evening. "But how would she break it to you? 'Hey, Dr M, I'm the daughter you didn't know you had. One of them. Yes. Now stop spilling that bastard nit-tric acid all over the -'"

"*Ni*-tric."

"She says nit-tric," Miller proclaimed. "Anyway … she'd say … oh, bollocks, I've lost my thread now. What I was meaning was … well … it's a sensitive subject. I think she knows."

"I don't."

"Will you shut up?"

"Sorry. It's just a sensitive subject."

"I know!" Mr Miller replied. "That's what I'm trying to point out. Sarah isn't going to come out with something as horrendously truthful as that all at once. I am pretty sure she knows. Look at the way she did it: came to *you* for help. When does that ever happen?"

"Never. Not even help in her homework."

"Precisely."

"Only because she tried to make me *do* her homework for her one time, so I told her to piss off and do it herself." He caught his elder's expression. "I said it more nicely than that."

Iain spluttered: "That's besides the fucking point, Russell! God, almighty. I wish you'd start acting your age. You're thirty-three, aren't you?"

Russ pouted. "Yes."

"Then shut up. Act your age. Sarah has been very devious in that she's trying to play devil's advocate with you. You need to play it back with her."

Dr Matthews sighed. "Nah. I can't be arsed. I'll just resign from the school and get out of her life."

"Andrew Jones, you're an immature individual. And … did she *really* puke on your dick?"

Tony slammed his head in his hands as he sloped on his bed. "I don't want to talk about it. I can show you if you want."

Sarah jerked her head across the room to where her brother was sitting, cross-legged and wide-eyed as ever. "You're just one big contradiction. Any other boy's penis, and I'd be there in a second. But you're my brother."

"No I'm not."

"Yes you are."

"No I'm not. Not by blood."

Sarah exhaled loudly. "As if that means anything."

"Apart from the fact that we can have sex. And that means you can see my dick."

She snapped at him, "Don't be a twat. Of course we can't have sex. You're my brother. You're adopted. That's like saying I could shag Dad, even though he's not my real father."

"If you liked older men. Who spend most of the day with their fingers up other women." Tony smirked at her, and uncrossed his legs, for fear he might not ever be able to use his genitals again. "Where is *she*, anyway?"

"The vomituous one? In my bedroom. Poised, waiting for your word to allow her back into your bedroom." She added dramatically but without emphasis, "And into your arms!"

"Whatever. Let her in."

"Yes, sir." Sarah started to walk out of her brother's room. "Hold on: does that mean you haven't washed your dick since last night?"

He just shook his head and lay back on his bed.

Sarah wandered back into her bedroom, found Hannah sitting morosely on the bed, and folded her arms. "You look like vegetables still exist," she kidded, not feeling remotely happy. "Tony wants to see you."

Hannah winced. "God, don't put it like that. That's what people say when you're in shit with teachers." She added, with feeling, "'Can I have a word, please?' Or 'so-and-so wants to speak to you.' Urgh," she shuddered.

"Well, you've obviously had experience," the other girl answered with a slight smile. "But my brother wants to talk to you, and that's about all I want to know." She went on, "That makes such perfect sense, doesn't it?"

Sarah pushed Hannah into her brother's room, neglecting at first to open the door and cracking her friend's head on the wood. With much effort, the shoving-process actually occurred. Pain on Hannah's behalf.

When Hannah found herself thrust headlong into the tussle of Tony's bedroom, she realised that she had nothing to say. She heard the door shut behind her - shut, not close - and looked back at it with a new word she liked to use: ominosity. Her head inched around. Her boyfriend, the one with the PENIS, was laying in front of her. On his bed. Flat as a Yorkshire Pudding. Well, it was Mrs Jones who did most of the cooking for her now.

"Yes?" he asked, in a rather curt manner. When he discovered that she wasn't opening her mouth and answering him, but not noticing that he had hurt her, he repeated, "Yesssss?" in a long and drawn-out manner that reminded her of one of her patronizing teachers.

"I'm here."

He didn't even look up. He continued to lay there, straight and flat and smooth. "I guessed that."

She swallowed a big lump of straw and made her way to his bed, a couple of steps away. She sat down on it, not knowing what else to do with this streak of piss she called a boyfriend.

Hannah looked over him. He had his eyes shut. She reached out a hand and touched his forehead, in a manner of stroking a pet rabbit. That doesn't attack you. "Tony?"

"Hmm?"

She continued to stroke him, her hand visibly shaking. "I'm sorry."

"Oh, forget about it. There's plenty of other times for you to do that."

She winced. "I didn't mean about that." Slowly, Hannah rolled up the sleeve of her black jumper, and she glanced only swiftly at the fresh blood she had forced herself to lose before pressing her arm against her boyfriend's mouth and chin, then running her arm across his face. There was just a little bit of blood. It dried tremendously quickly; she'd only cut herself with scissors so the cuts were rather shallow.

Tony slammed himself upright and touched the redness on his face. He pulled his hand away, his face registering horror and surprise in the worst way possible when he understood what had happened. He grabbed her arm, saw the blood and fresh cuts - and new ones that had healed from last night - and flung her away before getting to his feet with alarming speed.

"What the hell did you do this for? Why? Why?" Tony grasped her tightly, shaking her by the upper arms like on all good Jennifer Lopez movies. Yes, exactly. "We came to an agreement, didn't we? You wouldn't *do* this again! You wouldn't do this - " He broke away, letting go of her. She stumbled a little. Tony moved around his bedroom feverishly, wiping his face. "I can't believe you'd do this again! Why?"

That was it. Hannah began to sob. She collapsed on the floor and fell into the natural fetal position. She looked up at him, realising he was angry as hell, more irate than she'd ever seen him before and she had no idea how to stop him.

It took her a moment to understand that he was crying himself, but it didn't inscribe in her mind until he lost a few foot, on his knees, clutching her again. "Why, Hannah? Why?"

She sniffed. "I was sick on your dick."

"You cut your arm up because you were *sick* on me?" He muttered a "Jesus Christ!" to himself, glimpsing the bloody arm.

"I've done it worse before. This isn't even a grade B. D+, maybe. Pushing a C-."

He peered into her eyes, after moving her head. "You bloody lunatic," he managed to urge out a smile. She wiped his eyes once she had lost his grip of her good arm.

"So are you, crying."

"I wasn't crying. Hayfever."

"Cry-baby," she coaxed.

"I'm not crying!" he cried, laughing a little, more tears falling from his eyes. "I just care about you, that's all. I don't want you doing this to yourself anymore. I want you alive, whether you puke on me or not. And for both bad and good means." He exhaled.

Out of nowhere, although most likely from Sarah's bedroom, they heard: "Oh, bloody hell! Blood on my bloody bedsheets!"

A sad smile was exchanged between the pair. "Come lie on my bed. I'll get you a miniature towel so you can soak your arm and clean it up a bit. Hold on. I'll be right back."

Thirty-eight

Honestly, Men *Don't ...*

"Tony, I don't know how thick you actually are," Hannah could hear Sarah exclaim loudly in the adjacent room, "but men don't have periods. And there is no amount of alcohol or money in this world that would convince me otherwise. Well, maybe a million or three." A gap, where Sarah presumably inhaled. "So what really has been going on on my bed …eh?"

Hannah shut her eyes and lay down. She opened them again, fearing the dark lightness. Things could allegedly only get better. But then the old governments took that motto years back, and look where it got them. Imprisoned and cut up into little pieces.

Poor Tony. He was being verbally attacked by his sister, despite the fact that he was a foot taller than her. Hannah peered at her arm, on which the cuts were glaring at her with a straight expression, except for some that curved downwards.

It took her a while to notice that the phone was ringing. She got up, not knowing whether the phone would be in the hall-way or Mrs Jones's bedroom; the position kept changing and confusing her.

The phone tonight - or at least this *hour* - was in the hall. She picked it up. It was a slurring voice, someone who neglected to let her say "Hello" before he did. "Who's this?" the male voice asked.

"Hannah Simpson. Who's this?"

"Have I got the wrong nummer? Soz, sweetie. I wor wanting to talk to young Sarah there."

"Why has your voice taken on an Irish accent all of a sudden?"

"I'm Irish!"

She narrowed her eyes, opened her ears. "Is that Dr Matthews?"

"Uh-huh. Fooled ya', eh, dint I!" Manic laughter.

"Are you drunk, Dr Matthews?"

"Yes. Extremely. All that hydrocarbons and stuff … ol, ol, ol. Methanol, ethanol, blahblahblah. All have an O-H bond connected to a C. Carbon can make four bonds. I think. Oh, sweet mother of dog. Losing me mind, I am. Goodness gracious. Can I speak to Sarah? Pwetty pwease?"

Hannah put the phone on the table, and made her way into Sarah's bedroom, remembering to pull down her jumper arm so that her cuts wouldn't be revealed. Her boyfriend opened it the same time she touched it with pasty-white fingers.

"Sarah, Dr Matthews is on the phone. I'd be very careful. He's absolutely bladdered. He keeps saying stuff about O-H bonds. I can't remember much from GCSE, but I think he's making stuff up. As if Chemistry would be made up of that kind of crap."

Sarah thanked her friend and pushed past her.

"Hello?"

Which was always a good way to start a phone conversation.

"Ahoy, Miss Jones," came Dr Matthews' loosely tongued voice from the other end. "How be you this good even-ing?"

"Fine. What do you want?"

"So curt, Sarah, so *darn* curt. I was just wanting to speak to you seriously about something …"

Shit, it's that bastard practice assessment.

"Oh - er - sorry, Dr Matthews. I haven't had time to look over the sheet yet for the assessment. I … er … you know, what with me being in the hospital."

"Oh. Of course. Yes."

"What are you ringing me at home for, anyway? Did you want to speak to my mother?"

Dr Matthews hesitated. "Er … um … yes. Please."

"I'm not sure if she's in yet or not. Hold on two secs."

Sarah raced downstairs, found no-one, and sped back up to the phone. She held it to her ear. "Hello?"

Dial tone.

On the following morning - Thursday - Sarah trounced into school feeling that everything would be back to normal again. Bollocks. Just like Monday, due to Sarah's tardiness, a group had gathered around Maggie and were chuntering.

"So I said, 'You call that a dildo? Here, Andy, I'll show you where to stick it." Maggie demonstrated with her hands.

"You are *so* rude," Tom was saying, clasping his hands together. The polish on his nails was only just visible in a pale shade of bright pink. "Tell us more. What else did you and Andrew do?"

Sarah threw her bag on the table, breaking the non-silence with loud noise. "Listen, *Maggie*. I have had just about *enough* of you pretending to be me in order to make fun of me. Or get more friends. Or whatever the hell you're doing. I am fucking Sarah Jones. Well … I mean, I - myself - I'm not committing any sexual act with Sarah Jones because I *am* her. You are Maggie. I am Sarah. I have birth certificates, adoption papers to prove it."

Maggie chuckled. "I know I'm Maggie. I think you're going crazy, sis. I was just telling the group - Talullaah, Jenna, Tom, etcetera - how I shagged Andrew Cage last night."

Sarah stood there, still, her eyes boring in the evil chasm that was her sister. "I don't understand."

"When you get big enough," Maggie clucked, "you'll learn, *ma petite sœur*."

Everyone sitting around the Bitch began to crack up, as if her French was the most funniest thing they'd heard in years.

Sarah snapped back, "Well … fine then … *œuf-tête*," and sped to her locker.

Thirty-nine

Plotting

"Pissing bollocks."

That was Andrew's version of events. "I thought you were coming on a bit too strong."

He had had his hair cut whilst he'd been away yesterday; he was now the perfect image of a sex god … apart from the absence of needle-tracks. Sarah groaned as they sat together in the common room just before lunch-time. "God, this is all a load of shite."

Andrew sighed and looked at her. Just that.

"What?"

"Of all the minute numbers of days you've known your sister … haven't you learnt something?"

"She steals my clothes? And dirty knickers?" Sarah added quickly, "That second thing was a joke, by the way."

"No, Sarah. She lies. Lies and lies and lies. Look at the way she swapped identities with you on Monday! She couldn't swap bloody personalities though, could she?" He touched the front of his quiffed hair. He looked a little like Dr Matthews, actually, the way his hair was trimmed. Crap. "Come with me."

Andrew Cage grabbed Sarah's arm, and pulled her to the other side of the common room where her 'friends' were sitting, crowding around Maggie and listening to her tell fabrications of so-called truth. "… but we're off into town tomorrow night. Just to go fuck in one of the clubs. Just like my brother did with you, Marie." There was a pause.

Talullaah piped up, "Marie? What are you doing here? You're usually out at lunch-time."

Marie laughed a little. Sarah and Andrew watched on, as if peering through one-sided glass. "Well … it's not exactly lunch-time yet, is it?" The bell rang, signalling the longer break, and they watched Marie get up. "Besides, Tony Jones didn't even get it up me. Christ, what do you think I am? A fucking bucket?" She walked out.

Jenna and Talullaah exchanged glances. "Where the hell does she go every lunch-time?" Jenna asked, touching her slightly pink, short hair. She'd lengthened it with extensions … naturally, they'd fallen out.

"She always comes back looking exhausted."

Sarah decided that now would be the best chance to enter the conversation. "She, er, she's shagging Ben Dover the I.T. technician."

Several pairs of eyes glared at her. "What?"

Later that day, Sarah found Hannah counting money on one of the table-tops in the library. "Hey - you'd better watch out. The tree-trunk of a librarian has banned any cash over five pounds from in here."

Hannah looked up. She was wearing a white shirt today, seeming to Sarah like she was developing a taste in colour. Her eyes even looked blue. Probably due to the lack of false darkness. "Three ninety-seven. Bloody two pences. I hate them. *SO* annoying."

"Not as much as pennies."

"True, true," Hannah agreed. "Anyway … I didn't know you had a free period now."

"I don't. I'm skipping Dr Matthews' Chemistry lesson."

"Still pissed off about the father-thing?"

"Wouldn't you be?" Sarah shook her head miserably. "Plus, I haven't sketched out any ideas for the practice *practice* assessment thing. I don't even know what the bollocks he's on about. Molar mass this, atomic mass that. Chemistry teachers talk the biggest load of balls. Then they expect us to believe what they say."

Hannah smiled. "Do you really have to believe them, though?" She scraped her money off the table and into a hand. "Surely you should just learn the stuff. Who cares whether it's true or not."

Sarah sighed. "I suppose. But this father-thing. I want to talk to him about it. I just don't know how to approach him about it."

"Woah - you've suddenly changed your mind all of a sudden."

"What can I do?"

Hannah sucked on the corner of her bottom lip for a moment. "Hmm. I … I can't think. Surely there must be some way of catching him out."

"Catching him out?"

"Yeah. Surely you've realised by now that he knows."

"He knows?" Sarah echoed, before nudging hair out of her eyes.

Hannah noticed her hair-iness. She delved in her bag. "Here. A clip. Try putting it behind some of your hair." She added, as Sarah took the clip as offered, "Of course he knows. I just don't know if he knows you know. But at least he doesn't know that you know he knows."

"Just don't - do that."

"What?"

"Confuse me with *knows*. How do *you* know he knows?"

"He rang you last night. When has that ever happened before? Never. According to Tony, anyway. So … shit. That must mean he's presuming that you know."

"He knows I know he knows? Or he knows I know?"

Hannah sighed, then stopped, mid inhale.

"I've got it."

Sarah leaned in closely.

"You'll be sorting out your driving license, your provisional soon, won't you?"

"Yeah."

"The thing on the back, you have to get someone to sign it, and a photo. Someone who's known you for more than two years and who has some sort of a degree."

Sarah was glowing. "Someone who isn't family!"

"Exactly."

"There's just one problem."

"What's that?"

"He's not family. He's just my biological father."

"Just try it. It'll be blatantly obvious what you're doing, even if he refuses to sign."

"But what if he does sign it? What about corruption? The highs and lows of the collusion in the education system? Questions about truth and the truth about questions? Casual sex?"

Hannah giggled a little. "What's casual sex got to do with anything?"

"Just thinking about him and my mum having - urgh, God - urgh -!"

<u>Forty</u>

<u>The End?</u>

Friday morning. Chemistry time. Dr Matthews tapped his fingers awkwardly on the desk as he wondered when any of his students were going to turn up. It was getting on for half nine now; they were well over twenty minutes late. Fifteen, in fact.

His head was all scrambled up; he'd not had a lot of sleep last night. It was probably due to the permanent hangover he seemed to have nowadays. He opened his scarlet folder and tried to finger the date with long, stubby digits. He couldn't remember the date. Twenty-something of October.

The bell rang after one period of Chemistry passed. He looked up miserably, scratched his head, nudged his tie. His ears pricked up. Footsteps.

In marched Sarah and Jenna, looking as casual as ever despite their suits. Sarah. His daughter. Dr Matthews touched the paper bulge in his suit pocket with a heavy heart. He wasn't sure he was up to teaching this morning.

"What are you lot - you two - doing here so late? Where's everyone else?"

Sarah plonked herself down on the front bench with her friend. "Well … we were just pratting around," she grinned, "but everyone else who are insane enough to do Chemistry are also doing Biology. They've got a Field Trip."

"This early into term?"

"Actually, it's the end of half-term," Jenna piped up. She merged a smile onto her rash-covered face. Allergic reaction. "We break up today."

"Today?"

Sarah sighed, "Anyway. Can we do some work? I'm getting bored."

Sam Jones had lost David again. She eventually found him perched on the thick window-sill, panting and trying to write his name on the condensation-covered window. "You're such a naughty little doggy, aren't you?" she asked, lifting him up by his neck, failing, then bear-hugging him before David finally took the hint and ran towards the leather sofa, which he proceeded to empty his bowels on.

The door knocked. Or, at least, the head presumed, somebody knocked on it. "Come in!" she called, trying to shift the little dog from the seating area. It barked once and ran under her oak desk. Sam looked disdainfully at the faeces on the sofa and sucked on her bottom lip.

It was her daughter. Maggie Jones was brought in with a teacher whom Mrs Jones didn't recognise at first. It was Miss Moore, her hair cut neatly and in a complete mess. "Your daughter … your daughter is in *trouble*."

Sam Jones stood, sloped in front of the old oak desk. "Sarah? What's she done now?"

Helen Moore tutted loudly. "Mrs Jones, I think you need to tattoo your daughters with their own names. *This one*, *Maggie*, seems to be having an identity crisis. She thinks she's Sarah."

"Well, maybe she is."

"Mrs Jones, there's no use sticking up for Maggie. We all know in the staff-room about Dr Matthews being the father of the two of them. Quite frankly, I'm surprised, as I believe him to be a screaming bender - in denial - with no idea about women."

"It was only one *time*, Miss Moore."

"Well, there you go." The Languages teacher sniffed. "*This one* thinks that it is horrendously amusing to impersonate her twin sister to try and wreck her life. For instance, this one was overheard telling everyone she … didn't make it to the toilet in time … and therefore wet herself in front of Dr Matthews."

Sam Jones folded her arms. "Dr Matthews, Dr Matthews, Dr Matthews. Personally, Miss Moore, I think you have some issues with Russell. Leave Maggie here. I'll sort her out. Oh - and Sarah did have an embarrassing incident in front of the afore mentioned teacher. I think it was a little *quid pro quo*, however."

Helen Moore slammed the door behind her.

"Your fly's down."

"Excuse me?"

"Your fly's down, Dr Matthews. On your trousers."

Russ glanced down at his zip. "Er, thank you Jenna. Could you … er … be getting along now? I've got … er … another class to teach."

He wasn't quite sure where his stutter was coming from, but as he swiftly did up his zip, he saw that Sarah, the only other member of the class this morning, was standing awkwardly next to his desk at the front, perched on the edge of the lifted platform.

"Can I help you, er, Sarah?" he asked after watching Jenna prance off.

"Yes," she answered, wafting some paper in front of his face. "You've known me for more than two years, haven't you?"

"Yes …"

He scratched his forehead.

"My provisional. Here. I need someone with a degree, generally, who can sign this thing here," she pointed at her driving license form, "and the back of this photograph. To say it's a likeness of me."

"Oh!" Dr Matthews exclaimed, fetching a black biro. "I thought it was something else …"

"Like what?"

"I don't know."

He poised his pen over the paper. "I have to write my address down here?"

"Yes." Sarah laughed nervously. "Don't worry. All the pupils know the members of staffs' home addresses. They look them up on the Internet. Easy."

"I …" he hesitated. "I … okay." He started filling in his details.

Sarah tried to sound amiable but failed happily: "You're just not allowed to fill it in if you're a member of the family, that's all. You've got the degrees and everything."

Dr Matthews looked across at her with a slight smile on his face. "Well, good job I'm not family then, is it?" He scrawled his signature along the back, across the photo, and filled in the rest of his details. "Terrible photo, Sarah. Were you intoxicated at the time?"

"Er, no, Dr Matthews. I'm never intoxicated. I don't drink. Apart from at home," she lied. "It's illegal. Makes you do crazy stuff when you've had too much of it. Talking of doing crazy things when you're drunk, Dr Matthews …"

"There you go. All signed for. Done and dusted. Well, best be getting on. Speak to you later. Have a good weekend. And half term." He ushered her away.

At the end of the school day, Maggie Jones was still being held captive in her mother's study. She needed the toilet desperately; the urge was uncontrollable and yet her mother was firm in her decision: "You're not leaving this room until you explain your behaviour."

And since she was brought in here almost seven hours ago, her mother had only half spoken to her - once telling her not to slouch, another time telling the dog (David! What a common and un-canine name!) not to hump Maggie's leg.

Apart from that, there was silence.

Apart from the telephone calls. And the knocks on the door. And the computer beeps. Presently, Maggie was in the mode of standing up, walking around a bit, then sitting on the sticky leather sofa for a second with her legs crossed, then repeating the process.

A loud knock was heard. Maggie got up again, danced around, sat. She spotted that gay Chemistry teacher entering the large room, pulling out some paper from his suit jacket. An envelope. Or as the French called it, *une enveloppe*. He placed it on the desk in front of her mother, who was staring at the phone as if it was of some use.

Sam Jones glanced up. "Oh - Dr Matthews. How nice to see you before half term. I do hope all those *disgustingly* inaccurate photographs have been removed from each of the notice boards."

Russ peered at her. "Yes, Mrs Jones. Yes, thank you, they have. Did you ever find out the culprit?"

"It was your sister Lucy, Dr Matthews," the headmistress answered with a taut smile on her face. "Apparently she thought it would be visually amusing to broadcast false photographs, crudely photocopied, for the public eye to see."

"Did you punish her?"

"Of course. Don't think because you're a member of staff here that your sibling is going to get away with every wrong thing she does. Just … most of them, because nobody can ever pinpoint the blame on her. However, this time … she was stumped. Like every member of the former England cricket team before that horrible accident." Sam Jones sniffed. "It was quite simple this time. The librarian caught her. An anonymous tip-off. Krystelle-May."

"What did you punish her with?"

"I got her to take all the posters down."

"That's it?"

"Oh, and I suspended her until further notice."

Russ couldn't speak, until he said: "Okay. Well … that's besides the point. I came to hand in my notice. This *problem* with Sarah is just getting worse. I think she knows about me being her father."

There was a pause. "You have two daughters, Russell. One of them is sitting just across from you."

Russ jumped back a little when he spotted the *other one*. The Frenchie. He swallowed and scratched his head. "I … er … hi."

Maggie didn't reply. She was too busy dancing around, sitting, then dancing again to bother notice her biological father.

"Maggie … go use the toilet like other decent human beings would," her mother chided. Her second daughter ran out, but Sam Jones wasn't allowed another word out of her mouth before Sarah ran in, hair a mess and looking like she herself was trying to find a place to urinate.

"Mum, he can't be my father! He signed my provisional license thing! That's, like, illegal!"

Sam folded her arms. "Now, Sarah! You know they made it illegal to use that word nowadays!"

"What?" her daughter asked, perplexed.

"Never mind. And mind your tongue."

Sarah slowly turned her head to the left, where her teacher and/or father was standing. Sarah absently wafted the folded paper in her mother's eyes before dropping it on the table in front of her.

"He can't be my - he - er - um -"

"As I was saying, Mrs Jones, here's my resignation. I quit. As from now. I know I can't do that, but I am. There are … too many complications in the workplace for me to continue working here. Miss Moore, for example."

Sarah sank to the sofa, missed it, and landed on her arse. She got up and found the leather seating carefully. "You're leaving?"

He turned only briefly. "I'm leaving this place. I just … can't handle … rumours … and lies … and …"

"And responsibility?" Sam Jones asked, touching the resignation with her manicured nails delicately.

Dr Matthews shut his eyes, unbeknown to Sarah but witnessed by her mother. When he opened them again, the headmistress was positive she could see glimmers of tears in them.

Russ picked up the provisional license that Sarah had brought in and moved to where she was sitting. "I'm afraid this is invalid, Sarah." He ripped it straight down the middle, then again, and dropped the pieces to the ground. Dr Matthews walked out.

Sarah sat there, numb, feeling the tears roll down her face even before she wanted them to.

Sam Jones sat down in her swivel chair and clenched fists in her jet black hair. “Oh … bloody bollocks!”

www.ingramcontent.com/pod-product-compliance
Lightning Source LLC
LaVergne TN
LVHW052006160826
845678LV00005B/1670

* 9 7 9 8 3 6 3 1 1 8 5 2 4 *